BLUE MOON

literary & art review

Novel Excerpts – Short Stories – Poems
Paintings – Photographs – Reviews

Issue 12

Blue Moon Literary & Art Review

Founder: Scott Evans

Editor: Scott Evans
Assistant Editor: Adam Russ
Poetry Editor: Gayle Jansen Beede
Editorial Assistant: Carolyn Waggoner
Layout Designer: Josh Tulman

Cover photos: Jury S. Judge

Publisher:
Blue Moon Literary & Art Publishing
327 Twelfth St., Davis, CA 95616
www.bluemoonlitartreview.com
530.902.0026
Email: evans327@comcast.net

Short Stories, Excerpts, & Poems

Images

Interior Photos by Gayle Jansen Beede

BLUE MOON

Cover Artist: Jury S. Judge
Jury S. Judge is an internationally published artist, writer,
poet, photographer, and political cartoonist. She is the
cartoonist for The Noise, *a literary arts and news magazine.*
Her Astronomy Comedy *cartoons are also published in*
The Lowell Observer. *Her artwork has been widely featured*
in literary magazines such as Dodging The Rain, The
Tishman Review, Claudius Speaks, *and* Timber. *She has been*
interviewed on the television news program NAZ Today *for*
her work as a political cartoonist. She graduated Magna
Cum Laude with a BFA from the University of Houston-Clear
Lake in 2014. If you are interested in her artwork, email her
at jurysjudge@gmail.com.

The Accidental Casanova
by Martin Weiss

I still vividly remember a Sunday afternoon, a week after my eleventh birthday, when Grandmom took me on a long trolley car ride to a noisy, narrow Philadelphia street crowded with many Jewish-owned pushcarts and small retail stores. We entered a curtained doorway in a storefront located between a kosher butcher shop and a dry-goods store. It was dark and gloomy, the air heavy with the scent of incense barely masking the overpowering odor of fried liver and onions. An old, skeleton-thin woman no taller than me, clad in a red caftan, hair hidden by a red and gold kerchief, sat behind a table with a funny-looking deck of cards in front of her. Her face was deeply wrinkled, grotesquely made up with powder, rouge, Kohl, and bright red lipstick. Long, golden earrings hung from distended earlobes, and several bracelets of multi-hued stones jangled on her thin arms. She made a garish contrast to Grandmom, severely dressed in black. The lady and Grandmom spoke in a language I'd never heard before, but I knew it wasn't Yiddish. Grandmom told me to shuffle the deck, which was hard to do because the cards were oversize and my hands still small. The lady then dealt out the cards and moved them around, re-shuffled, then moved them around some more. She talked in that strange language to Grandmom, who kept asking questions and getting answers she didn't seem to like. I remember the words "Dybbuk" and "Koorvah" (whore) were mentioned several times, because Grandmom's reaction each time was to exclaim, "Oy Gevalt!"

The lady took my hands and scrutinized my palms very carefully, still talking to Grandmom. When the lady finished, she leaned back, patted me on the head, and pinched my cheek. Her expression was more grim than friendly. She then took the stub of a pencil and a piece of scrap paper and wrote something down. Grandmom took the paper then folded it small enough to fit into her change purse. She gave the woman three one-dollar bills, and we left for home.

Almost two years later, I was studying for my Bar Mitzvah ceremony. My private tutor was the sexton of our synagogue, an old, bent-over man whose white beard and breath smelled of both garlic and cigars. He was teaching me Hebrew and preparing me for my readings of the Torah when I became thirteen years old and recognized as a man according to Jewish tradition.

One day, Grandmom interrupted us and started a discussion in Yiddish with the tutor. She handed the tutor that slip of paper written years ago and spoke forcefully to him. He nodded his head in agreement several times and turned to me, placing the paper so I could read it.

"Do you know of Kabbalah, young man?" he asked in his heavily-accented English, "or of Jewish mysticism?"

"No, sir," I replied.

"He is too young," the tutor said. "He is still a child. Maybe in a few years."

"No!" Grandmom insisted, "He must be told now. It's for his own good."

I could tell from his expression the tutor was reluctant to continue, but he replaced the paper in front to me, flattening out the folds, and said, "Read these four names aloud and commit them to your memory. Never to be forgotten".

The scrap paper, written in Hebrew by the old woman said, 'Agrat Bat Mahlat, Lilith, Naamah, Eisheth Zenunim.' I could read and say the words only one syllable at a time.

"Do you know who or what this says?" he asked.

I shook my head no.

"Your grandmother says these words were given to you by a lady who told your fortune and read your palm. Do you remember?"

"Yes," I answered.

"These are the names of the four Angels of Prostitution, the Wives of Satan. Do you know what all that means?" he asked.

"No," I replied.

The tutor and Grandmom got into a heated discussion. The tutor kept saying, "He's too young," and Grandmom kept saying, "Soon he'll be a man. Tell him now. He must know."

Stroking his beard for a moment, the tutor then said, "Jonathan, these are the names of four very evil women you might someday meet. They might have different names, but if you do meet them, run away. I warn you here and now. Have nothing to do with them," he said, shaking his index finger at me.

I looked at his face and that of Grandmom. Their expressions were as frightening as the warning. "If they have different names, how will I know them?" I asked.

"Smart lad," the tutor said, patting my head. "You will know them because they will tempt you into doing something you will later regret."

It was too confusing for me. I didn't understand what this was all about. But I knew it was important to Grandmom, so I said, "I promise. I will stay away from those ladies."

Grandmom fed me Jewish paranoia with my baby food. She was an uneducated widow from a small village in Czarist Russia and now lived in my parents' house. I'm Jonathan Mark Sturn, born at St Luke's Hospital in Philadelphia, PA on September 30, 1937, the only child of Rifka and Max Sturn who owns a moderately successful 'Ladies Corset Shoppe.'

Grandmom's justifiable fears were borne out of generations of persecution, depredation, and slaughter of the Jewish community in the Old Country. Pragmatic to a fault, she anticipated receiving the same treatment upon reaching the allegedly gold-paved streets of America. She lived with the certain knowledge the powers that be, meaning her Christian neighbors, anyone in uniform, any government representative, and other unknown, sometimes mystical forces, would inevitably assail her family specifically, and the Jewish people in general.

Her defenses against this were many and mysterious, including small, red ribbons strategically placed in out-of-the-way locations like under a crib mattress or intertwined in shoelaces. She lit candles and employed strange hand signs, secret potions, and whispered prayers. But the defense in which she believed and tried to teach me was behavioral control. I should just follow certain time-tested rules: don't call attention to myself; don't make waves; don't deviate from the established (Jewish) path; and above all, don't mix with or trust the Goyim. Failure to follow those rules would get me the attention of the Evil Eye and its terrible retribution. Her methodology of instruction involved instilling fear and terror. In other words, she scared the shit out of me when I was a kid.

"What happens if I'm bad," I asked Grandmom once.

"Take my word for it; you don't want to know," she answered in Yiddish, a language that made it sound even more foreboding and scary.

With both Grandmom and Mom brainwashing me into believing there was an "Evil Eye" looking over my shoulder just waiting for me to transgress, it was no wonder I grew up a tentative kid. Unfortunately, as I was growing up, there were plenty of times things happened to prove them correct, which gave me more than a touch of anxiety.

There was also another reason for my paranoia. Every time I ventured outside what were the safe boundaries as defined by Grandmom, parents, culture, or ethnicity, I paid a price, one way or another. Trouble or trauma always seemed to dog my smallest step into a non-traditional or wayward path. Like the time I wrote the love note to a sixth-grade classmate.

Two of my sixth-grade classmates, Jeannie and Sheila, fought over something or other. Jeannie then asked me to write an unsigned Valentine's Day love note to Sheila. All I had to do was write what Jeannie dictated and address the envelope. She would get a stamp and put it into the mail.

"Why have *me* write it?" I asked, uncomfortably aware her request might involve a no-no.

"Because you are positively the last person anyone would think would write a love note," Jeannie replied.

Since this was the first time in six years of school that cute Jeannie had paid any attention to me, I was anxious to please her—that and because she had the biggest breasts in our class.

"Will you let me touch your breasts if I write the note?" I asked.

Jeannie didn't hesitate for a moment. "Sure," she said, "but only the left one, and not until tomorrow."

So, I dared the Fates. As neatly as possible, I wrote the note she dictated, though not quite understanding all the terminology Jeannie supplied. She even had to spell some of the unfamiliar words for me. I then copied the address she gave me on the envelope, leaving off any return address.

The next day I approached Jeannie in the cloakroom, my right hand eagerly expecting the reward.

"I changed my mind," Jeannie said, "You can't touch my breast, but you can carry my books."

"Never mind," I replied, secretly glad I didn't have to touch those mysterious but magnetic bulges.

Five days later, the principal of the elementary school, Mr. Charleton, called me to his office. When I saw the love note and envelope in the center of the principal's desk, I felt the grip of steel fingers clutching at my stomach. They twisted tighter when I saw the expression on his face. I swear the Evil Eye was glaring at me from over his shoulder. I had a flashback to Grandmom and the tutor warning me about being tempted by a female into doing something I would regret. Could Jeannie be one of those evil women? Nah, I concluded, she wasn't old enough.

"Did you write this? Don't deny it. Even a blind man would recognize your terrible handwriting. What possessed you to do such a stupid thing?" he asked, without pausing. "When Sheila's mother brought it to me, she wanted the writer thrown out of school and tossed into jail. I calmed her down and promised to punish the evildoer. The only good thing I can say about this 'love note' is that it has perfect sentence structure, spelling, and punctuation. You must be paying close attention during Miss Dunlap's English lessons."

"Thank you," I said sheepishly.

"It is also very erotic. Where did you…"

My confused look must have puzzled him.

"Do you even know what erotic means?" Mr. Charleton asked.

There was a long pause, during which I could see myself getting beat up daily by my irate mother and then by the tough kids in reform school where I was sure to be sent.

Mr. Charleton let out a long sigh of patient exasperation and then placed the love note and envelope in the top drawer of his desk. "You have to be punished," he said, "for stupidity, if not for anything else. But this is your first serious offense in six years, and you will be graduating soon, I'll take it easy on you. I won't tell your parents, but this is what you must do. Starting tomorrow and every day until next Friday, you will bring to my office the following sentence, 'I promise everyone I will not do stupid things anymore,' written neatly, three hundred times. Is that clear?"

"Yes sir," I gulped, happy that my parents wouldn't be told and that I wouldn't be asked about Jeannie's part in this. All in all, I felt lucky. Funny thing, Sheila later bragged she had received a secret love note for Valentine's Day from someone she described as a handsome high school senior.

10

Jeannie, on the other hand, made it a point to invite Sheila to a sleepover party. Both girls ignored me for the rest of the term. I never got to touch either one of Jeannie's breasts.

At the graduation ceremony, Mr. Charleton handed me my sixth-grade graduation certificate, shook my hand and said, "Make sure you don't forget your promise, Casanova."

I didn't know who Casanova was. When I later found out, I decided it had been a compliment.

Marty Weiss is the author of this excerpt from his unagented and unpublished adult coming-of-age novel, "The Accidental Casanova." In it, encounters with adultery, embezzlement, and murder help Jonathan Sturn find love, maturity, and success in a complex social and business environment.
Marty has had fiction and non-fiction articles in numerous publications, including The Sun, The Good Old Days, *Philadelphia regional newspapers, and Sunday magazines.*

11

2017 Jack Kerouac Poetry Prizes
Poems selected by Dr. Andy Jones

First Place

Yo, Top Diggity Deity
by Julia Levine

i'm not asking for sleep
inside the burned out
charred up rubble
where the homeless
roast sewer rats
over ayn rand novels
while the rich sit
in their wine cellars
watching hurricanes
line up in the atlantic sea
like black friday shoppers
outside target—   no me
i'm after something
to bake & shake us awake
to the small fortune
of our watery planet
spinning around the rim
of a black hole—
& while you're at it
boss-a-nova big-cheese   please
make it an intervention
like the ones for drug addicts
my daughter watches on tv—

you know the show
where after years
of cooking up meth
& sleeping with bad johns,
the family members
read their letters
that begin with love
& end in urgent pleas
for the madness to stop
while the addicts
throw their damaged hair
around angrily
but eventually lay their faces
in their hands & sob—   shit
i'll even be the rehab counselor
if you make me the teeth of prophecy
my mouth the size of creation—   listen
this weather is sick as a dog
as in fundamental mental
as in our entire state
is not just golden
but literally on fire
as in dire
& the deregulations
& deformulations
& de-tyrants
sticking their metal straws
down deeper
into the black gold
& sucking it up
from the last wild holdouts—
has me so bad off
that last night in my dream
i held a match to my poems
& threw them burning
into the river

thinking   art   fart
what good is rhyme
in the end of times?—
but they were real bombs
exploding the levies
the fisherman and stoners
tumbling into the flare
and concussed boil
of my nightmare
while i ran from there—   hey
chief one on high
i swear sometimes at night
i can hear the stars
that trail behind our earth
crying like children—
and if you are the mother the father
they say you are   please help
our one and only messed up
blessed world—
i'd give my front tooth
my left breast
my itty bitty body
to save this heavenly one—
but look here
your holiness of humankind
seek & you shall find
that even in my own mind
i stood bereft
at the earth's deathbed
burning my poems my prayers
& all it did
was hurt the water instead

———————————

Poet Julia Levine delights readers and listeners alike with her humor, insight, and poetic flair. Levine has won the 2015 Northern California Poetry Award for her collection, Small Disasters Seen in Sunlight; *the 2003 Tampa Review Prize for her collection,* Ask; *the 1998 Anhinga Poetry Prize and bronze medal from* Foreword *magazine for her first collection,* Practicing for Heaven, *as well as a Discovery/*The Nation *award. Her latest poetry collection,* Small Disasters Seen in Sunlight, *inaugurated the Barataria Poetry Series for Louisiana State University Press in 2014. Her work has appeared in several anthologies, including* The Places That Inhabit Us, The Autumn House Anthology of Contemporary American Poetry, *and* The Bloomsbury Anthology of Contemporary Jewish American Poetry. *Levine earned a PhD in clinical psychology from UC Berkeley; she lives and works in Davis.*

Untitled
by Trina Drotar

Beautiful ran.

Chased.
    Sought nested rested fed.
Ran toward the river's edge,
  to where the cormorant had once been seen, high in a tree,
black wings spread for drying against a blue sky shadowed
by the branches surrounding the one upon which it perched.

A lone bee hovers, places pollen grains in its sac,
moves as a helicopter around the flower's core,
dipping in, returning to hover state.

Footless. Wingless. Finless. Furless. Featherless.

A worry stone is a living rock.

Have you ever witnessed a leaf's birth?

A woman said she would allow her cat to become pregnant so
          her children could witness kittens being born.
Another woman suggested a documentary instead.

A leaf unfurls.
Leaves do not simply appear full-size on trees.

A rock tumbled across and down the street, somehow avoiding cars and trucks and people riding bicycles without helmets. It made its way from intersection to intersection, unaware of the meaning of red, yellow, or green. What it sought is unknown. Where it originated is unknown. That it was alive, those who encountered it would find themselves in agreement. A man tried to capture the rock, but it slid into a pile of other rocks. Broken rocks. Crushed rocks. Rocks that had been discarded. The rock was soon on its way again. The rock was spotted in a pile of orange, red, and yellow leaves on one street, cooling its underside on a green expanse of lawn surrounded by iron gates on another, and at the bottom of a shallow pond on yet a third.

Bees swarmed the house,
    covered walls, windows, emitted a buzzhum,
                could not exit.
    Bodies filled the fireplace.
An old man climbed a ladder,
      sprayed.

People gathered, entered the house.
    Looked.
      Snapped photos.

Asked about the living.

Trina L. Drotar is a literary and visual artist and workshop instructor in Sacramento. A writer, editor, and publisher, Drotar is active in the literary and visual arts community in Northern California. She is on the advisory board of the I Street Press and the Poet Laureate Park project, past board member of the Sacramento Poetry Center, and former editor of both Poetry Now *and* Calaveras Station. *She has more than 20 years of editing experience, and more than 30 years of writing and art experience. She wrote the column, "Book Talk," for* Sacramento Press, *co-hosted the reading series Crossroads, and coordinated several Sacramento 100 Thousand Poets for Change events in 2012. Her work has been widely published, received multiple awards including the Dominic J. Bazzanella Literary Award, and her artwork is held in collections worldwide including in the Museum for Women in the Arts in Washington D.C. and Sacramento City College.*

>45

by Anara Guard

What is greater than forty-five?
The stars in a smallest corner of the sky
Stars on the U.S. flag

Trombones in the big parade
and keys on a piano

Any mountain, anywhere, anytime
The Statue of Liberty's height
My height

Teeth in a shark's jaw
Bones in the human body
Eggs laid by a common toad
Days a child grows within the womb

Bottles of beer on the wall
Cards in a deck, even after we remove all the jokers

Colors in the big box of crayons
Native American nations

Body temperature
Boiling temperature
The lines on the 1040 tax form where you must total up your
income tax and your payments made

Number of days that the Montgomery bus boycott lasted
And months of the United Farm Workers grape boycott

Your zip code
Age of our republic
The call numbers of every public radio station

The price of freedom
The cost of justice

The Dewey call numbers for all books
    on history, literature, science, technology, psychology,
philosophy, politics, religion, language, journalism, travel,
and art

        What is greater than 45?
Whether measured in length,
    width,
            height,
                    depth,
                            time,
                                    temperature,
                                            frequency,
                                                    price,
                                                            span,
                                                                    count,
                                                                            cost,
                                                                                    distance,
breadth,
        duration,
            or significance,
        what is greater than 45?
                            We are.

Anara Guard grew up in Chicago where her first job was tending the corner newsstand for a penny a minute while Carl-the-Newspaper-Man ate his lunch at Steinway Drugs. She later worked in a thrift shop, pharmacy, check clearinghouse, food co-op, community radio station, small town library, as a maid at a resort on the shores of Lake Michigan, and as a self-defense teacher for women. Anara studied writing at the Urban Gateways Young Writers Workshop of Chicago with Kathleen Agena, the Idyllwild School of Music and the Arts with Norman Corwin, Columbia College Story Workshop, St. Joseph's College with Stu Dybek, and the Bread Loaf Writers Conference with Robert Cohen and Alix Ohlin. She graduated from Kenyon College in Gambier, Ohio, and Simmons College Graduate School of Library and Information Science in Boston. In 2010, Back Pages Publishing issued her first collection of short stories, The Sound of One Body. *Remedies for Hunger (2014) is her second collection and was named one of the Best Books of 2015 by the* Chicago Book Review.

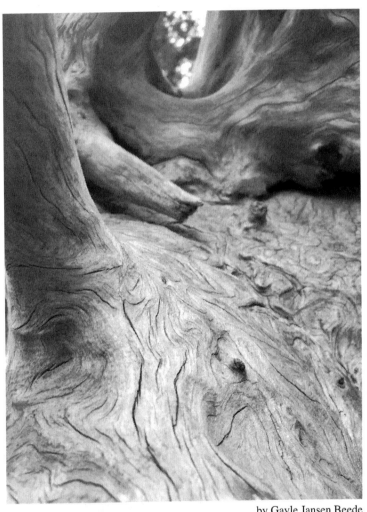

by Gayle Jansen Beede

Three Poems
by Barbara Link

Montana Wheat Field

I stand
half a yardstick high,
grasshoppers spring into my cupped hands,
Dad counts heads of hail-damaged stalks.

Suddenly,
rattler, rattler, rattler,
clicks like tap shoes on a car roof,
flat head,
polished agate eyes,
a coiled hemp hose braided with diamonds,

tail like Salome's hips.

An angel of a snake.

I think of frogs moving through the snake's belly,
dissolving like bar soap in wet fingers,
first the leaf-green skin,
then flaky white flesh that tastes like chicken,
then putrid yellow lungs, burping air,
rosebud heart,
last the lace-white bones.

Dad grabs a broken shovel,

strikes,
slicing head from eight-foot body,
brown and yellow kaleidoscope:
the hard earth,
Dad's khaki pants and straw hat,
the linen colored wheat and dust on my shoes,
the broken handle of the shovel,
dried mud on the

rusty blade.

Edges

Stunned by the smell of cut grass
I stop.
Watch the mower whirring, whirring,
Leaving long, skinny, windrows,
Of green.

Suddenly, it's every summer of my life.
Again
I'm nine.
Jan and I sit on the hot curb.
Suck grape Popsicles,
Tongue the drips
From our dusty arms.

Later we beg for a sleepover
In our screen porch.
We roll out sleeping bags,
Fat green armyworms
Dropped from trees.

After dark we sneak out
In seersucker PJs.

Flitting into backyards and gardens,
Clumsy ballerinas.

We crunch gritty carrots.
Fence with stalks of pink rhubarb.
Slap arms and legs,
Stinging wet whips.

We dash the warm sidewalk
To the last block in town.
A vacant lot, waiting for
Wet cement, fragrant wood, ringing hammers.

We perch on the fresh-dirt-basement-hole,
Dangle feet over the edge.
Our fingers grip the dirt clods,
As a huge black and white sky wheels above.
We're terribly, terribly small,
But not afraid.

Road Trip

Stunned by 5 a.m.,
I wait on summer-wet-grass while
Dad ties suitcases on station wagon rack,
Rubs his bristled cheeks.

I carry my stuff in Grandma's
Embroidered pillowcase.
A deck of blue and white playing cards,
Corners torn from playing violent slapjack.
A fringed leather marble bag,

Clinking with seventeen silver dollars.

I perch in the back seat between sisters,
Pinched if I touch their legs with my dirty sneakers,
Or kick the front seat.

We start in Montana shivers,
Window hot air by North Dakota.
In gas station restrooms
I crouch over seat-less toilets.
City Park for lunch,
Cold wet plums, tuna sogs into
Rainbow Bread.

Afternoon stops for road repair,
Tan like dirt on construction worker's arms.
We loop around army convoys
Streaming to summer camp.
Whistles from soldiers for my big sisters.
They fluff their hair, wave lovely arms,
Wind blowing through white sleeveless blouses.

Stupor hours.
Mom's head collapses on seat back,
Turquoise chiffon scarf over curlers,
Like tiny silver garbage cans.
Sisters lean on sides of car,
Sleeping mannequins.

Dad and I listen to baseball radio,
"A high fly ball to left field."
I rest my chin on the back of his seat.
Sniff dusty, sweat and Old Spice.

Tires roll on asphalt, our first divided highway.
Almost there.

I chant--Harmon Killebrew, Vada Pinson, Pee Wee Reese,
And like a long string of pink bubble gum,
Pull out the moment—
A girl alone with her dad.

*Award-winning California author and poet, Barbara Link,
has had three stories aired on KVPR, a National Public Radio
Affiliate. Her poetry and fiction have appeared in numerous
literary magazines and small presses. She also received the
Sacramento State University Bazzanella Prize for fiction. Her
memoir,* Blue Shy, *was published in 2010 and awarded first
prize in the Sacramento Friends of the Library First Chapter
contest. She co-authored* Coffee and Ink, *a handbook for
writing groups and was a past editor of Sacramento's* Poetry
Now. *In addition, she was a poet/teacher for California
Poets in the Schools for over fourteen years. Most recently,
she was awarded second prize for poetry at the Mendocino
Coast Writer's contest. Partial list of publications:* American
River Review, Poetry Now, Mindprint Review, Anima,
Missouri Review, Women's Compendium, Hardpan, Earth's
Daughters, (2014-2016) Whitefish Review, Dead Snakes,
Noyo Review, Piker Press (on Dec 5, Dec 12)

The Well
by Anne Da Vigo

In Nazareth, a cistern nestles
Beneath the carpenter's house.
It's cool here, dark, mysterious
Where winter's rain is hidden
To be carried outside in the hot season.
Water for the wheat, the pomegranate tree,
The dry tongue.

Mary lowers a bucket, draws it up
With a strong, brown arm,
Pours it, watching the rivulet
As it sinks into the powdery dust.
Months will pass before she plucks a pomegranate,
Lets the blood-red juice stain her fingers,
Crushes the soft seeds between her teeth.

Anne Da Vigo is an occasional poet who has published short stories and a novel, Thread of Gold.

Three Poems
by John Dorroh

The Corona Effect

1.
I was sitting with your mother in front of
Brenda Lee's house when the moon began
to pass between us and the sun. She saw it first—
the robin that fell from the tree, a red blur,
a rock, falling 40 feet from a branch,
startled by the sudden change in available light.
2.
We scurried to the sidewalk's edge, expecting to see
its bird skull crushed onto the ground, or wings bent,
broken, functionless
like the leg of a sprinter with a bruised calf.
Her wings were beating, stirring the air and dust
into a frenzy, just inches off the ground, like a blender,
a fury of orchestrated confusion. "I'm outta here,"
she seemed to say, flying up, up into the waning sliver
of light that left all creatures
somewhat confused.
3.
Your mother said, "I'm sorry," then asked me later
if anything strange had happened in the front yard,
or was it only her bird brain, her dementia
blocking out the light, casting a bright
white corona around her precious head
that none of us could observe without protection.

Blackberry Train

The Greenville & Santa Fe pushes its metal chest across
the fenced border of our back yard where the blackberries grow thick
in miserably hot southern stagnation,
blackberry ballerinas hanging onto tough prickly stems,
resisting yanks and pulls from little hands and fingers that bleed
with great regularity.

Arms moving swiftly, frantically orchestrated eddies,
my sister and I racing to the patch,
each with a favorite bowl:
mine, a well-worn funeral-green Tupperware,
its lid stretched to an improper fit from overuse;
Barbara with the glass Pyrex that Mama warned would get heavy,
that she'd drop it and spill her seeded treasure into the dirt.

The July sun, a magnified eye of white fire, slows down the dance.
We are oblivious, images of blackberry cobbler in our heads,
jam and sweet ice cream from the hand-cranked machine
on lazy Sunday afternoons
when neighbors and cousins visited and sweated on shaded porches.

The train lunges forward
into the gray, misty evening, returning tomorrow
like yesterday and the day before that.

French Lesson

The French have a way of advertising
life by the color in their fields: fuzzy
purple rows of lavender, yellow mustard
plants, unbelievably dark green stalks
of leeks and lettuce so lush you could
lose your children in it.

I ate their throbs of life – not just the
essence – entire veins, savoring
each bite like a dying man who might
pass in the night. No excuse for leaving
untouched bread or cheese that took
years of aging; for claiming that anything
needed anything: salt, pepper, God forbid,
croutons, unless they put it there themselves.

These are not barren lands, au contraire;
rich folds of full-bodied creams; butters,
unadulterated, pure and sweet and full
of love. The blues are not about the food.
Art abounds and if you cannot claim it
and touch it and taste it, then you might
need lessons which I am happy to give.

The verdict is still out whether John Dorroh taught high school science. He showed up, however, every morning at 6:45 with at least two lesson plans in his briefcase. His poetry has appeared in Suisun Valley Review, Dime Show Review, Sick Lit, Indigent Press, Haiku Journal, *and others. He also dabbles with short fiction and rants.*

Pyro
by Gayle Jansen Beede

The Sandy River was once named the Quicksand River by Lewis and Clark, and it joins the Columbia fourteen miles upstream of Portland. Back in the day, Native Americans established villages on floodplains and seasonally gathered huckleberries, fished for salmon, and hunted deer and elk along this river. For a while I let my mind wander and imagine the life a Native American woman would have led. We're here, after all, to wind down and to beat the heat, but dipping into cold water to cool off is one thing, when you've got a condo to go home to. It's another thing altogether when that river is also your laundromat, your cooking water, your bathtub, and your highway.

It's crowded today, and for good reason. Portland, typically drenched with rain, is in the throes of a record-breaking heat wave. I have a rash on my arms to prove it, my skin's way of protesting. We've come to a spot that's less popular—not the most scenic fork of the river, but Joshua chose it for the view of the train trestle, and because of the numbers of birds we might see in the surrounding trees. On days off, we like to get out in nature if Josh isn't on call for the ER. Sunbathing, bird-watching, train spotting: our idea of R & R.

"In case you're wondering why I'm playing in the sand, I'm trying to enjoy what's left of my childhood."

Josh gazes up from the paperback he's reading to look at the boy who's just plopped himself down on the sun-scorched sand right next to us. I glance around for his parents, and find no sign, as I rub sunscreen onto my arms and legs, looking forward to cracking open my own book. But I admit, this kid's got my attention.

"So, are you a local?" Josh asks, stifling a laugh.

"I live in three places. Portland, Gresham, and Idaho. I like Idaho best. Portland is too much city."

"Too much city. I like that. You have a way with words. I'm a doctor, so I've heard a lot of fancy language. Why three places?"

"My mom and my two aunts take turns parenting me."

"Ah, now that's an arrangement. What's your name?"

The boy stops digging for a second, shaking sand from his hands and then rubs his forehead. "Oh, I don't tell people my real name. I go by Pyro, because I love fire."

"That sounds kinda dangerous." I find a leaf to use as a bookmark. "Do you want to be a fireman some day?"

"No. That would be boring. I want to do something with destroying buildings."

He resumes digging and sculpting, all of his lanky limbs involved.

"Oh, like demolition." It's the first thing that comes to mind when he said *destroying buildings*.

"Yeah."

"But not with people in them, I hope." I adjust my sunglasses to get a better look at this kid without July's unusually bright sun glaring in my face.

"No. That's terrorism," he says.

"You're right, it is. So, Pyro, how old are you?" Josh enters the conversation again, having cast me a look that said listen up, this kid's onto something.

"I'll be thirteen in April. Girls liked me until about a year ago. They were all over me. Not any more. They call me Igor, you know, Dr. Frankenstein's assistant." He poses in an imitation of Igor. "My brother is one year older. He meets people, but I don't. It's really annoying. He goes off with his girlfriend—" Pyro smirks—"it gets me depressed."

"Wait, you know the meaning of that word, too? I

don't think I did at your age, but things are different these days."

"Yeah, what, do you think I live in a cave or something? Anyway, I have to watch them make out. I don't need to go through that." He scrunches his face into a sour expression. Josh and I chuckle.

"Hey, it's not funny! More like... gross."

We straighten the edges of our towels and settle back into position, me with my book, Josh unfolding a map of the area.

"So what kind of doctor are you?"

"I work in the Emergency Room. That's where you don't know what kind of problem you'll solve next. People come in with all sorts of maladies and injuries. Burns, bicycle accidents, motorcycle spills, even gunshot wounds sometimes."

"I know what an Emergency Room is. I was there when my brother accidentally stabbed me. We were making models, and the X-acto knife gouged my arm. Sometimes I think he did it on purpose. See?" He holds out his left arm to show off the zipper-like scar. "So, can you fix everybody?"

"I certainly try."

"My uncle is a veterinarian. One time he had to amputate a cat's leg—it got mauled by a lawn mower. But I hate cats," Pyro continues. "They trick you into thinking they're awesome. I've done some research, and I found out we're related to dogs. I kept clicking on the computer, and so, if you'll happen to notice, that's why people like dogs so much."

"Hmm, that sounds crazy to me," Josh says. "You sure you're not making this up?"

Looking around, I see he has a point, though. There are almost as many dogs splashing in the water as there are people.

"Well, never mind about the dogs. Did you know that when hummingbirds are dating each other, their wings beat 200 times a second? And once, when I was looking up *de-*

36

molition, I found the word *demonology*—you should've seen some of those pictures! I kept clicking on the computer, and that's how I learned to build my first tunnel." He digs for a while, falls into the hole to see how he fits in it, climbs out, digs some more and jumps back in. "Pretty soon, *you'll* fit in it," he says to me. "Oh, I'm not saying you're fat, just tall."

He hits water at the bottom of his pit, and then a rock.

"I've done some more research, and I found that sand came from rock. It got broken down into a million particles."

"That's called erosion, isn't it?"

"Yes, ma'am, it is." He tosses me a wink.

"Do you have a drama department at your school?" I can't help but ask.

"Yeah, and my mom makes me go to it. I *hate* it. I don't like being watched."

"But it seems like you'd be so good at it. How about musical instruments, do you play any?"

"Flute, recorder, and a round thing with four holes—" he demonstrates with his hands how it's played—"not the sideways kind, that's the girly way."

"I bet you've already tried your first cigarette," I say. He's brought out the mischievous in me.

"Nope. My mom smokes. That's bad stuff. She wants to quit. She can't help it. At one time she could, but now she's addicted." Pyro burrows into his deepening sand pit, bending his legs and using his arms like oars to shove loose sand into the hole, half burying himself.

"You could hide her cigarettes."

"I did one time, but I won't any more because she'll make sure I get grounded, and getting grounded sucks. She won't let me read books or use the computer. I could care less about TV. Besides, we don't have one."

"What about your dad, does he smoke too?"

"Beats me. He left us a long time ago. My mom used to have a picture of him on the dresser, so I know what he looks like, but she took it down. We have a closet where he left some of his stuff, like his army duffel bag and the head of a deer, and the Mauser rifle he shot it with. My mom keeps the closet locked, though, because with me and my brother in the house, she doesn't think it's safe." He stops digging for a minute, raises his arms straight up, and twirls them. "I might try to find him, though. Maybe he lives somewhere near the end of this train line."

"What about your friends? Are they as curious as you are?"

"Oh, I gave up friends. All they are is trouble." He's buried to his chest in sand, only his head and arms can be seen. "You think I could breathe under the sand if I covered myself all the way?"

"Well, for a while you could," Josh says, "because the texture of the sand is somewhat porous. But if I were you, I wouldn't try it."

"My mom probably wouldn't even miss me if I got smothered—"

"Whoa, now why would you say that? I bet your mom would be devastated if something like that happened."

"She's usually paying more attention to my brother because she's afraid he's going to run away. Oh, hey, look!" He scrambles out of the pit, sending sand flying all over us, and bolts for the trestle yelling, "Here comes my train!"

"Precocious kid," Josh says, sitting up to feast his eyes on the filthy Burlington Northern Santa Fe engine at the head of the freight chugging across the bridge. "Seems starved for conversation."

"And attention. Jesus, look how fast he's running, Josh." In half a minute, the boy's cheetah stride has carried him to the pillar of the trestle where I see him stop to catch his breath before he begins to climb the support. "What the hell is he doing?"

"Good God, stay here and watch our stuff." With that, Josh takes off running, faster than I've ever seen him, including the mornings I'd time him when he was training for his first marathon. We'd brought a pair of binoculars, for zooming in on branches and identifying birds, so I pick them up and bring them into focus on the boy. My brothers had an Erector Set when they were kids, and this is what the gigantic trestle reminds me of. You've seen them, designed kind of like roller coasters, bolts and beams and metal supports I don't know the official names of, but this feisty kid is climbing up them as though he were part gibbon.

What I hear is shrill screeching, like a sawmill at full volume, hissing, mechanical squealing. The trestle appears way too flimsy to support the freight's tonnage (I'm no bridge designer, I'm a graphic artist whose job is to embellish the ordinary), and clearly there have been countless trains that have traveled across it before. But the crew in this one has evidently spotted disaster, a wiry kid now on the level of the tracks, and blows its deafening horns. Is it actually attempting to stop? The train is so close, its engine so loud, it's impossible for Pyro to heed Joshua's absurd warning—he's waving his arms and apparently screaming at the top of his lungs at the boy from below—and then, of course, it occurs to me that Pyro knows full well what he is doing. Silly me, thinking my husband a hero: Pyro is a thrill seeker. Inside that spindly body lives a ravenous, insatiable, possibly volatile little daredevil.

I never have been a daredevil, living instead within self-imposed boundaries where I can fool myself into believing the world's a cozy place. When I was four, my mother became deathly ill, spending weeks at a time in the hospital, and so I was taken to live with my grandparents who could take care of me while my father was at work. Those long weeks remain fertile participants in my life's thirty-five year old chronicle. Memories, like old friends, show up on the doorstep of my mind's porch—the smell of Oma's Tabu; the clink of my own tiny teacup of coffee, its bitterness sweetened away with more sugar and cream than any child should rightly consume; and most poignantly, the trains. Dear God, those trains.

Oma's and Opa's backyard gate opened to a field that spanned to the train depot. Their house was so close, sometimes the windows rattled when trains chugged or zoomed by, and at night, hearing their ferocious deep-throated chug, it was as though they were living creatures, and I was devoured by something I could not name, held captive in a land where loneliness shook hands with fear and pulled me into its dungeon. For Christmas one year I was given *The Boxcar Children*, Opa's attempt at softening my view of the monstrous, industrial beasts.

So when I first met Josh and he revealed his boyish addiction to trains? Let's just say I hardly shared his mania.

Through the lenses I see him now, at the foot of the trestle, reaching into his pocket for his cell phone. If I know him, he's calling the hospital to alert them of a potential patient and to get the trauma team ready. A gutsy twelve-year-old is about to lose his legs. Or even worse.

I know little about the physics behind the force of something as colossal as a moving freight train, but I can tell you I'm letting off my own fierce steam by screaming now too, drawing a crowd around me, all of us standing, some of us jumping up and down as we try to fathom the sight of Pyro nearly being blown off the bridge as he hops onto a boxcar. It's smeared with graffiti, so my eyes are distracted. In a fit of disbelief, I drop the binoculars, pick them up and wipe them free of sand. When I peer into them one last time, I see in the wide open door of the boxcar that Pyro has found his footing and is waving, the wingspan of his long lean arms like the plumage of some rare, rare bird.

Two Poems
by Gayle Jansen Beede

Trying To Meditate

I should be able to learn from the memory
of my Nana's lemon meringue pies.
Parts becoming a new whole.
Egg whites whipped into stillness,
congregation of yolks in waiting,
an omniscience of sugar.
Lemon's sharp juice squeezed from
its source with firm, manicured hands.
The making takes every bowl
she owns. Her apron tied
in a flawless bow, chores finished,
hardworking husband due home,
she pulls herself away from the black
and white screen of the Zenith TV
where news of Nazis
overturns her entire sense
of things. She casts a prayer
through tears while pinching crust
into perfect high flutes,
pouring all that's sweet
into one place, carrying it ever so
carefully across the kitchen,
placing it gently into the oven.

The Beautiful Culprit

after Jean-Paul Sartre & Simone de Beauvoir

thighs touching
under the table

wit issuing from lips
burning neon tips

of cigarettes, smoke
& talk filling Cafe Flore

crowded with minds & bodies
promiscuous ideologies

uttered between sips
of apricot cocktails

& seductive stares
into bedroom eyes,

post-war bliss
partly to blame

for the flame,
yet existence itself

is the beautiful culprit,
tangents of jazz

minor notes undulating
in subterranean clubs,

Simone's hands
sneaking beneath

Jean-Paul's black
woolen turtleneck

Blue Moon's *Poetry Editor, Gayle Jansen Beede is the author
of* The Beautiful Culprit, *a compilation of stories and poems;*
Audrey To Zoe: An Alphabet of Critters, *a children's book;
and a poetry collection titled* You Can Practically See Cattle
Dancing.

by Gayle Jansen Beede

Two Poems
by Ken W. Simpson

A Monument To Mediocrity

Home was a room
with four walls
a floor and ceiling
where omens hid
in a closet
full of cliches
and insecurity thrived
on a diet of bias
and white lies.

Clashing Cymbals

Dissonance is the reason
the tune began
with a plea from a flute
for joy to merge
with the sound of a violin
but ended instead
with a crude retort
from a temperamental tuba.

Ken W. Simpson is an Australian poet whose collection and memoir, The Incoherence of Bliss & My Life in Orbit, *has just been published by Cholla Needles (US). A chapbook,* Waving at Strangers, *was published by Fowlpox Press in August, 2017. A collection,* Patterns of Perception, *was published by Augur Press (UK) in January, 2015.*

Winter Sunday
by Timothy Robbins

Enough wind to stir the
firs outside my window,
not enough to blow fine
snow from the roofs.
I'm listening skeptically
to Beverly Sills trill, "Sweet
mystery of life, at last
I've found you!" Sunday's
no Sabbath when faith and
work run out. Still, through
some vague but powerful
habit of feeling, it's cozier
under this blanket than it
will be tomorrow morning.
Seven chimes from the Arts
and Crafts clock in the
living room stir an image
of the hours my dad spent
building it, alone in the garage,
hot from a wood-burning
stove, listening to Terry Gross.
Fifteen minutes later the first
Cambridge Quarter invokes
quiet hours working at his
elbow. The half hour brings
the January he photographed
me feeding ducks on ice,

recalling my attraction for
surfaces that crack. Third
quarter: It's the 1970s. He
hangs a tangle of Christmas
lights above his and Mom's
pillows, hooked to the radio,
blinking to Disco hits.

*Tim Robbins teaches ESL. He has a B.A. in French and an
M.A. in Applied Linguistics. He has been a regular contribu-
tor to* Hanging Loose *since 1978. His poems have appeared in*
Three New Poets, Slant, Main Street Rag, Adelaide Literary
Magazine, Off The Coast, *and others. His collection,* Denny's
Arbor Vitae *was published in 2017. He lives with his husband
of twenty years in Kenosha, Wisconsin, birthplace of Orson
Welles.*

Chipmunk Life
by Kim Cope Tait

Without a doubt,
I write it down
so that it will
become a part
of the landscape
of my memory.
So that in some way
I will know
who I was—here
and as part of this
scenery. I want to
admit everything
that shames me,
relinquish what aches
in my acacia heart.
I don't try to ascertain
the number of pauses
in our conversation
or the ways I have
disappointed you
even now.
I just continue in my
way, words tucked
into the insides
of my cheeks.
Chipmunk daughter,
chipmunk wife,

chipmunk life.
Bushy fan of a tail
rising behind my body
as I go. The moment
reveals itself to me
as one of clarity and
consciousness,
but I still can't sort
the grain from the chaff.
Words rise to the ceiling,
along with the soft panting
of our kind. Language
is everything, and it
is also simply the one thing
you utter to save yourself
each moment.
The way to live,
even so.

———————————————

Kim Cope Tait's work has appeared in literary journals and magazines in the U.S. and abroad. Her chapbook of poems called Element *was published in 2005 with Leaping Dog Press. Her full-length book,* Shadow Tongue, *is forthcoming with Finishing Press.*

Safety Drill
by Judi Calhoun

It was 9:05 one morning my first-year teaching, when my principal, Matt—a balding, Bruce-Willis-type—came strolling into my art room to whisper covertly that today our school would be conducting a safety drill and that I should be prepared.

Needless to say, it's vital that public schools like ours remain well-prepared for any disasters. Unfortunately, I personally had little experience with the practical application of how this type of drill played out. Was my Bruce Willis look-alike going to pull a Die-Hard maneuver on me or the school? Or was I expected to brandish a weapon? Um, yeah. I envisioned myself throwing my body in front of my students—what teacher wouldn't, right?

"Relax," said Matt, when he saw my puzzled expression. "It's easy. Lock all the doors. Pull down *all* the window-shades, and keep the students quiet till it's over."

Yup, piece of cake. I could do this. I stood a little taller and saw a vision of Washington crossing the Delaware River, standing against the Hessians forces in 1776. I could handle every class that came into this room... except maybe one— Kindergarten!

Everyone is in awe of the lion tamer in the cage with half a dozen lions. Everyone but a kindergarten teacher.

Although I have no idea who first penned this, it is true, extremely true... scary true.

As Bruce Willis strolled out into the hall, I glanced over at the long bank of windows. In other classrooms, it might be easy to roll down the shades, but not in my room. You see, I happened to share a classroom with the Music department, and since storage was a priceless commodity, we tended to utilize every square inch of the room, and then some.

Piled up in front of the bank of windows lived an assortment of rolling carts, a thick metal rail pushcart holding twenty music stands, not to mention the gargantuan-sized wooden guitar rack, and one oversize speaker. All of these things stood in the way of reaching the six tall windows. The white old-fashioned shades were curled around themselves near the ceiling. Probably some janitor cleaning windows over summer neglected to draw them back down.

Mind you, I'm no spring chicken, but I consider myself agile, maybe not agile enough to climb Everest, but skilled enough to scale two flights of stairs from the office to the cafeteria in about twenty seconds, give or take. Good enough for the American Gladiator competition? Probably not. And to be honest, I could never see myself scaling a wall or hanging from ropes.

Throughout my morning, I started to stress about it. When were they going to pull the alarm?

At an age when so many friends had retired, I was developing curriculum, grading projects, setting up chairs, dragging tables, scraping paint from places paint should never be, and lugging heavy boxes to and from my car—all the glamorous perks of a low paying teaching job.

On snowy days as my husband drove, I was trying not to think about all those glamorous perks. Maybe they were the reason I grit my teeth every time I viewed posts on social media from former schoolmates relaxing on some Caribbean beach, or waving from an exotic cruise-ship deck. I chided myself for the jealousy, and then quickly reassured myself. *I am doing something important. I am making a difference in the world. Giving students hope that they can accomplish anything as long as they believed in themselves—right?*

I ate a hurried lunch in my classroom amid shifting supplies, and as usual had just enough time to swallow my sandwich before fifth grade started lining up outside my door.

No alarm sounded—yet.

As fifth grade waved goodbye, Kindergarten came bouncing in all chattering, chairs scraping as they found their seats. I started wondering if it was too late to change the curriculum. Maybe have them just do some coloring pages, no doubt, one after another, until they'd exhausted my entire supply, because of those two little words that every art teacher dreads hearing, "I'm done." They shout them out with a heroic smile on their smug lips, like it's something good.

The planned curriculum: a painting project, with water-tubs, paint-brushes, tempera cakes arranged in a plastic pallet (colors no longer identifiable), and disseminating papers dripping wet with black or mustard-colored mucky mess.

Of course, it would have been a nightmare rearranging the classroom. I mean, months ago when I'd prepared the lesson if I had any idea about a safety drill. But I was jumping to conclusions... or was I?

Everything went so smoothly, it was going to be the best class, ever. Every student, including my 'troublesome three star' students were working quietly. It was a little slice of heaven... until the alarm sounded. Class erupted into chaos of shouting, "What's that? What is that?"

Nerves rattled, I bellowed above the din, "This is just a safety drill. No need to panic. Remain calm. Just continue painting quietly."

I rushed to the doors first, locking them and drawing the shades. As I turned toward the bank of windows, one by one my students got out of their seats, "Mrs. Calhoun, what are you doing?"

Naturally, I tried to explain, which garnered more questions. The moment I started moving heavy equipment, they thought it was a new fun game and all suddenly wanted to 'help'.

What was that line from Kindergarten Cop? *"You know, kindergarten is like an ocean. You don't want to turn your back on it."* Well, for me, that was a most accurate description of the chaos loosed, and some briny deep trouble crashed down into the classroom.

All those precious cubs were out of their seats; all of them—natural and free—spilling water buckets, swinging paint brushes loaded with red, blue, and black paint. A few aspiring artists decided my desk needed a new paint job, a rather bright red and pink to be exact. While other students climbed up to the sink, turned water on full throttle and gloriously splashed in it, emptying the soap dispenser. The students not running around were grinding up pencil erasers in the electric sharpener, just because it made an interesting sound.

And last, but certainly not least, were a few kind students, with hearts of gold, 'helping' by repeatedly banging the carts into my step-ladder, throwing me off balance, nearly tumbling me.

It was like watching midget circus performers from my high perch, and like Queen Elizabeth, I shouted orders.

So much for remaining quiet.

Returning to my former glory, the Gladiator clambered up to great heights, practically scaling the wall, stretching on my tiptoes, hanging by a tiny thread, just to pull the window shades (I did this six times!) I could hear the roar of the crowd applauding, or was it just the wild creatures below?

The moment I got every shade drawn, climbed down, the loud-speaker erupted in a tone followed by an announcement the safety drill was over.

As I inspected my class, my students all covered in red paint, in their hair, across their cheeks like Scottish warrior extras in the movie *Braveheart*, a knock came on the door. It was our kindergarten teacher. I unlocked the door and when she stepped in, I let go a loud sigh.

The look of horror on her face said it all.

With her help, my students cleaned up, well some of them did anyway, others were still messing with that wretched pencil sharpener.

As I bid them farewell, as always, they rushed at me, lavishing me with love, telling me that this was the best class, ever! Can we do this again next week?

The perks and rewards of teaching are many. Like when I am out shopping and run into my students, they run with arms wide to bless me with more extravagant hugs. During class, they gang up on me for a group hug, and leave messages on the board telling me I'm their favorite teacher. In those moments, I think to myself, *who needs a sunny beach when you're given this much love.*

And yes, I would take a bullet, for every last one of them.

Judi Calhoun lives with ferocious black bears and wild wolves that howl at the moon every night in the Great North Woods of New Hampshire. She is a fiction author and member of N.E. Horror Writers Association. She creates short stories that have appeared in many e-zines, recently Hungry Coyote, *published by* Portable NOUNS, Crimson Street. com: J.L. Rymer, Theme of Absence, *several stories with* Great Jones Street, *just to name a few. Her fiction short stories are published in multiple texts such as* The Haunted Coach, Concord Coach Anthology, *by Plaidswede's popular pulp fiction series:* Murder at The Monitor: *EMP Publishers,* Blood Hunter; Visual Adjectives, Superhero Anthology: Sweeney's Dark Tale, *Great Old Publishing, Pernicious Invaders Anthology*: Invocations; High Tea with Ancient Gods *and many more. She is currently seeking representation for her YA novel* Dragon Girl.

"Blue"

by Scott Evans

On the west side of Highway 101 stood a series of hills that looked inviting, so I crossed the highway a block from the Fosters Freeze, and headed west through a neighborhood. The road eventually wound upward and curved toward a wooded area before coming to a dead end. But a trail appeared to lead into the trees ahead, so I followed it.

The path was well worn and eventually took me upward and into a clearing at the base of a much steeper hill. A small walking bridge allowed me to cross the stream and on the other side, the path simply ended. I continued up the hill and saw a herd of cows grazing over the rise. They took no notice of me and I wasn't much interested in them, so I continued climbing westward.

An outcropping of ragged black rocks stood at what I assumed was the top of the hill, but once I reached the formation, I realized an entirely new range of hills — small mountains, really — rose beyond. But I was tired by then, so I climbed up to the top of the rocky outlook and sat down.

The north end of Willits lay below me like something out of a picture book. The neat little houses lining the roads, two churches with white steeples, the buildings along Main Street, the lumber mill with its large conical smoke stack beyond — all of it laid out as if someone really had designed the town.

I could see what I later learned was Pine Mountain — the tallest of the small mountains on the eastern side of the valley. Seeing the lay of the land from this perspective somehow gave me hope. Pittsburg was a city on rivers between mountain ranges, and Willits was a small town in a wide valley between two sets of mountains as well. I didn't feel at home yet—not by a long shot—but I felt less like an outsider.

After about an hour or so, I headed back down the hill. But when I got to our cottage on Pearl Street, I still didn't feel like facing Mother again—she'd want to talk me out of joining the football team—so I walked to the end of the street toward the railroad tracks. There was a small horse pen between the end of our lane and the tracks. Candy was standing at the fence, feeding something to the old white horse inside the pen. In her faded pink t-shirt and frayed cut-off blue jean shorts, she looked older than fourteen, especially with her wild red hair. The horse was a sad looking animal, its sway back drooping as though it had carried a six-hundred-pound rider most of its life. Its mane was tangled and dirty, and the legs above the hooves were covered in mud.

Candy was startled when I walked up behind her.

"Hey," I said, "what are you feeding him?"

She glared at me at first, but then her expression softened. "Just some old carrots my mom threw out."

"Poor old horse. How long has he been here?"

"For as long as I can remember. Me and my sisters used to try to ride him, but we could never catch him. My stepdad slapped the hell out of me when he caught us chasing Blue around the pen."

The horse bristled as I stepped closer and tried to stroke his snout.

"Blue?" I asked. "Is that his name?"

"Don't know. It's just the name we give him 'cause he seems so sad. And when he was younger, his coat looked more light blue than it does now."

I tried again to pat his nose, but he backed away.

"Here," Candy said. "Give him this and he'll warm up to ya."

She handed me a limp carrot and I held it out. The

60

horse eyed me sideways but then stepped to the fence. It took the carrot and chewed it slowly. I noticed the green water in the trough next to the simple wooden shelter.

"Man, that water needs to be changed. It's slimy."

"Yeah," Candy said. She let out a long sigh. "They got a faucet over there. Sometimes I put fresh water in, but until somebody really cleans that trough, the water's just going to stay dirty."

"How can the owners neglect this poor animal so badly?"

"I seen an elderly man here a few times, droppin' off fresh hay and oats. He's all crippled up and it's hard for him to get around, so maybe it's just too much work for him. I don't know."

Blue's front shoulder shivered to ward off some flies. They buzzed around but landed back where they had been, at an inflamed scratch in the horse's flesh.

"That cut looks nasty," I said.

"Yeah. I wiped it off with some water yesterday, but it don't look any better."

"Keep him here a minute. I'll get alcohol and a rag. Maybe if we clean it, it'll heal up faster."

Candy gazed at me, as if she didn't understand. Or maybe she didn't believe me.

"I'm out of carrots," she said, "so I don't know how much longer he'll stay. He don't like people, mostly."

"Well, do your best. I'll be right back."

I trotted to the house and grabbed the bottle of alcohol and cotton balls. Then I went to the kitchen, took a red apple out of the crisper and sliced it into quarter pieces. Mother was asleep on her bed.

"Here," I told Candy. "Feed him one of these while I rub this alcohol in."

She took the apple slices and held one out. I leaned against the wire fence and tried to reach Blue's wound with a few balls of cotton that were dripping with alcohol. When

I finally touched the wet cotton balls against Blue's shoulder, he startled and ran off.

"Damn it," Candy said. "What if he don't come back now? What if you scared him off for good?"

Anger and frustration filled her voice. Too much to be normal.

"He'll come back," I whispered, trying to calm her. "Hold out another piece of apple."

She glared at me again. "Okay, but you don't try to clean that wound, okay?"

"I won't," I said. "But it sure looks nasty."

Candy turned to the horse and held a piece of apple out. "C'mon, Blue. Come get a nice piece of this here red apple." She made a couple of sucking noise, trying to lure the horse back, but he just stared at us. "C'mon, fella. Get some apple."

Blue turned away and faced the railroad tracks. A train was coming from the north, chugging out of the train yard slowly at first. Two engines appeared, picking up speed, and then a series of brown freight cars began rolling by.

"It ain't no use now. He won't come back."

"Why don't we try walking around to the other side of the pen and get closer. Maybe he'll come then?"

She considered this for a few seconds. "I don't like goin' on that side where all the blackberry bushes is. My sisters and me seen a rattlesnake in them bushes one time. All coiled up, ready to strike. So we backed outta there and ain't been back since."

"Well," I said, "what if I walk ahead of you?"

She grinned a lopsided grin. "Don't you know nothin' about snakes? They always strike the second person on the path."

I scratched my head. "I've never heard that before."

"Well, if you're gonna live 'round here, you better get to know about snakes." She gazed at the scraggly clump of bushes. "There could be a whole nest of 'em in there, for all you know."

It was harder to hear her thin voice now that the train had picked up speed and the freight cars were rattling by faster and faster.

"Well, then," I said, "let's go to the back side of the pen."

She laughed. "You mean, alongside them railroad tracks? Now? With that train barreling by?"

I scanned the back of the pen. "There must be three or four feet between the railroad tracks and the back fence. We'll have plenty of room."

Candy shook her heard. "There's only one thing scares me more than snakes, and that's trains. You know they come off the tracks sometimes and kill folks. You know that, right?"

I stared at the train. It was a long one, but I expected the caboose to come along any minute. "We'll wait until it passes, then."

"I don't know. I'd better get back inside. My stepdad will be waking up soon, and he'll want his coffee."

I looked at my watch. "He's just waking up now? It's almost four in the afternoon."

"He works the graveyard shift at the mill. Sleeps during the day. I already got into trouble this morning for playing my records too loud."

"Oh," I said. "Well, give me the apple pieces and I'll go over."

Again, she gave me a skeptical look, but she handed me the apple. The pieces were turning brown.

I walked around the south side of the pen, along a narrow dirt road that seemed to have been a continuation of Pearl Street originally. I turned north and walked between the passing train cars and the rusty fence of Blue's pen. Once I reached the northeast corner, I held out the apple slices. Blue eyed me but stayed put.

"Come on, old horse. Come get some apple."

His large watery black eyes stared at me with suspicion.

"I promise I won't try to clean your cut, old Blue. Come on over." I clucked a couple of times, but Blue turned and stepped away. "Well, here you go anyway," I said, tossing the apple slices at him.

When I glanced over at Candy, she had turned and was walking slowly to her house. Her head was down. It seemed as if feeding Blue was the best part of her life, and she dreaded whatever awaited her inside that house.

Scott Evans holds a Master's in English from the University of California, Davis, and teaches at the University of the Pacific in Central California, including fiction writing and a course titled "Crime, Punishment and Justice" that introduces first-year students to criminology from various perspectives. Before returning to California, he taught at Louisiana State University in Baton Rouge, which is one of the settings in his "literary" murder mysteries.

In Search of Fat City

by Howard Lachtman

Readers who can't bear to say goodbye to a book after they close its pages are the kind writers depend upon for immortality. Those who keep a book in their heart as well as on the bookshelf ensure a writer will not be forgotten.

Such loyalty is a worldwide phenomenon. Jane Austen fans, for example, come to England from all corners of the globe, hoping to find traces of immortal Jane at Chawton and Bath. Fans of Margaret Mitchell's Tara and Harper Lee's Mockingbird venture to the American South while "Gatsby" tourists search for their favorite Jazz Age lover and loser on Long Island. And if ever you chance to stroll down London's Baker Street, don't be surprised to find Sherlock Holmes aficionados wandering in a kind of detective fever, seeking the doorway of the mastermind sleuth's domestic agency at 221-B.

Some of these enthusiasts travel to cities you would not normally associate with literary immortality. Stockton, California, for example. Have you ever heard of Stockton? Karen Schoemer had.

"Stockton will always be a place that I first entered through the pages of a book," wrote Schoemer, a reader enamored of Leonard Gardner's Central Valley classic, "Fat City."

Schoemer found a lingering magic in the only novel Gardner ever wrote. She wanted to get close to the source and the author. So the Hudson New York resident and travel writer crossed the continent and put her boots on the ground for a tour.

Once in Stockton, Schoemer ignored such usual tourist points of interest as asparagus and tamale festivals, wineries, boating and sightseeing in the San Joaquin Delta, action at the Stockton Ports ballpark or a Stockton Heat hockey game, or the picturesque campus of University of the Pacific, where history was made on June 1, 1957, when University of California at Berkeley track star Don Bowden, arriving just in time from university exams, ran the first sub-four minute mile on American soil.

What Schoemer wanted were the sites—visible and, if possible, accessible—of Gardner's 1969 novel. She'd read the book. She'd made the trip. She even managed to snag Gardner as her personal tour guide. What more could a "Fat City" fan want?

Accompanied by a New York Times photographer assigned to capture the scenes of her Stockton pilgrimage, Schoemer had everything she needed to play the book-loving tourist mapping the landscape of a classic.

Fat City 2

Well, almost everything. Even with a living author at your elbow, she found, a quest of this kind can be problematic. For one thing, Stockton does not provide "Fat City" tourists any pamphlets or guided tour connection to the novel that made it famous. With its focus on the lives of marginal boxers, field hands and others on the low rung of the socio-economic ladder, "Fat City" is not high on the list of tourism promotions.

Schoemer's determination to go on the hunt raises an interesting issue. Can a reader enter more deeply into the heart and soul of a favorite book by standing on the ground that inspired it?

California does provide notable opportunities for readers seeking such connections. One can visit Steinbeck's Cannery Row in Monterey, explore the Carmel sea-coast house of poet Robinson Jeffers, retrace the San Francisco footsteps of Hammett's hardboiled Sam Spade and go back a century in time inside the restored writing room of Jack London at the state park that bears his name in Glen Ellen.

Visitors to these and other sites can sometimes be pleasantly surprised by the unexpected. Visiting Tor House forty years ago, for example, I was startled when I saw Jeffers himself seem to step out of the shadows. Was it a ghost? The supernatural moment passed when the figure was introduced to me as Donnan Jeffers, a son who bore an uncanny resemblance to his father, including a shy modesty.

The past also came alive for me on a visit to the Jack London State Park, where the spacious office of the writer had been restored in all the faithful detail of that early twentieth-century workspace. One could not fail to note here the adjoining desk of wife Charmian, a helpmate who did all the typing, manuscript preparation and mailing for a busy husband who divided his time between writing and farming. Stepping into the past here, visitors gained not only a glimpse of an efficient fiction factory, but also the secret of how London managed to produce so many books in a short life of forty years.

With Gardner at her side to trace the genesis of his novel, Schoemer was confident she could excavate "the lurid and legendary Stockton of Fat City."

What she found was that time and the city had moved on. Poverty and blight endure, as they do in many cities, but The Skid Row of Gardner's youth—the specific genesis of his novel—was long gone. The city fathers of Stockton are in no mood to plant memorials around what remains.

Schoemer was hunting for whatever she could unearth in her role as literary archaeologist. So she and Gardner spent a long weekend in search of what she called "extant landmarks and relics." Though few survived, Gardner dutifully pointed out a few landmarks noted in his novel—a faded hotel here, an abandoned property there, the open-for-business Xochimilco Café, and boxing great Enrique "Yaqui" Lopez's Fat City Boxing Club where aspiring pugilists still work on jabs, hooks, footwork and timing.

Was it enough to provide the visitor what she had hoped to find in Stockton?

Not quite. Schoemer wanted more. Perhaps what she really wanted was what every Gardner fan wanted—a sequel from the novelist in whose hand alone lay the key to the lost city.

Fat City 3

"Why didn't you want to write another novel?" she asked, echoing fans who have asked the novelist that question for more years than the 82-year-old Gardner cares to remember.

It was not a question Gardner wanted to hear again.

"I'm sure I *wanted* to," Gardner replied testily. No doubt he assumed that a personally guided tour of the wrong side of town in which he grew up would prevent that pesky question from being asked.

But even if he had wanted to, what would the novelist write about? He could hardly improve on the book he'd done—a book that has taken its assured place on the shelf of California classics. And having lived for so long out of Stockton, Gardner had little connection with the city of today except for an occasional visit to greet old friends and new readers, as he did with a 2017 appearance and talk at the Friends of the Library Bookstore. It was there that one "Fat City" fan shared her interpretation of the novel's innate message: "Be kind, for everyone you meet is fighting a battle of which you know nothing."

Gardner's only novel said it all simply, eloquently and memorably. He left his characters where he wanted them, in a timeless landscape. As a one-novel novelist, he quit the game with a knockout.

Schoemer appears to have made the best of the situation. She claimed she found what she was looking for in the space between "the tangible world outside and the inner layout of the mind."

Never mind that that space sounds more like limbo than a place on the map. She went home happy. Maybe Gardner did too. At the end of the tour, Schoemer noticed him "holding a pocket notebook that I didn't even know he was carrying, and he was writing."

Writing what? She didn't ask and Gardner didn't tell.

But one can't help wondering. Was the author making notes for a work about a novelist haunted by a fan who wanted more of him than he was prepared to give? Or a memo to himself about the hazards of guiding visitors in search of a literary landscape?

Of course, there is a far easier way to find "Fat City" than searching for relics and ghosts. Simply open Gardner's novel, begin to read, and you are there, in a fictional city more authentic and enduring than the one that was.

Why has the novel, originally published in 1969, remained a staple of modern California literature?

In his carefully crafted account of life in the margins and shadows of Stockton, Gardner portrays the boxers, field laborers, dreamers, drinkers and drifters he knew from his youth. The result is a book that involves readers with its off-beat characters, renders fight scenes with the crisp authority of one who has thrown and taken punches, and captures the truth of human nature beyond the square ring.

Fat City 4

"If I hadn't grown up in Stockton, the book wouldn't have been nearly as good," Gardner once told me. "The fighters I got to know at the Lido gym were farm workers. I got friendly with the fighters, most of whom were really nice guys, some of them barely making ends meet. How much harder a life could a guy have than being a pro boxer and a farm worker? What a way to make a living!"

Gardner never expected to make a living from his writing. Begun in San Francisco State College's writing program, the novel took him four years to complete. He was unprepared for its sale and prompt optioning by film director John Huston, for whom he wrote the screenplay.

"You never think it could happen. I just wanted to get a book published and think, gee, I'm a writer. That seemed like it would be so great. But then every magazine and important paper started giving it good reviews. And the movies bought it before it was even published. It was like a young writer's fantasy come true."

Although fans of the novel have long hoped for (and sometimes requested) a "Fat City" sequel, the author told me he had no intention of returning to the Fifties milieu of Billy Tully and Ernie Munger, the hard luck pugilists whose misadventures illumine the world in which they live to fight and fight to live.

"I ended their stories. It feels right that they remain in that time when they were young men, desperate to achieve something meaningful in their own eyes. They are really striving against the odds, and the odds were so stacked against them. I like where I left them. I think I should leave them there."

The quiet skill, humor and sympathy with which Gardner traces a pattern of human desire and delusion is enviable. There is unexpected poetry in his pages, such as Ernie's Stockton homecoming on a Greyhound bus "through the night coolness of low delta fields, past dark vineyards, orchards and walnut groves, isolated lights of farm houses, irrigation ditches full of moonlit water, and then on the outskirts, a gigantic Technicolor face speaking silently on the screen of a drive-in movie."

The magic evaporates the moment Ernie steps off the

bus, enveloped by heat and fumes, and moves through a depot of somnolent passengers, eager to pursue his idea of the good life. Will it be different this time? Or is Ernie deceiving himself once again? Welcome to Stockton. Welcome to Fat City.

A retired columnist, reporter and editor, Howard Lachtman was honored by The Stockton Arts Commision "for 24 years of superior reviews and commentary on the performing and literary arts in Stockton, as published in the record." He is the author of "Sherlock Slept Here." *(Carpa Press), a history of Sir Arthur Conan Doyle's travels and lectures in jazz age America, and edited the first Collection of Jack London's sportswriting in* "Sporting Blood" *(Presidio Press), the author of numerous short stories, including the prizewinning* "Memo From Human Resources" *and* "The Greeks Have A Word For It," *Lachtman's worldwide travel stories include the prizewinning* "Italian Style" *and the recently published* "Quebec To Key West: A Touch Of Frost, A Taste Of The Tropics."

by Gayle Jansen Beede

Borders and Boundaries
by Bill Pieper

The chopper came over low enough you could feel the downdraft, bullhorn speakers blaring in the heat. "Crew Five! Buzzard Point! Pull back and cover! Breakout's runnin' square up on ya'! Pull back and cover, now!"

Lately, if he had the dream, that was where Mike would wake up, like he just had, not even panting anymore. Other times, it would last until the worst part, thirty seconds later in the dark envelope of his reflective shelter, when someone had grabbed his ankle, dragging him back just as a heavy, crackling thump shook the ground right where he'd been.

Nearly losing his gloves, wrists cut and scraped from the shale-like rocks, he had yelled "Hey, fuckhead! Cut that out!" at whoever was dragging him, and couldn't guess what was happening or why. All he could do once the dragging stopped was huddle in tighter under his shelter, choked by his displaced helmet strap. Instantly he'd smelled and heard the fire sweep like a rabid animal through the low scrub on the ridge, and his skin sensed its passing broil.

After several endless, black, airless minutes, Derek, a CDF pro like the chopper pilot, had begun shouting. "Up and out guys, grab your tools if you can! Bunch together and head back how we came. Take a count. Be sure we're all here." Shaking, Mike had stood among a cluster of other rosy-orange protective suits. His McLoed had been in the shelter with him.

Behind them, on the nearly bald summit, the cross-rush of flames from what was a crown fire in the canyon be-

74

low had already self-extinguished against a yard-high rock fin. Intense heat can make its own wind, something they'd all been taught and that Mike had seen before. Out beyond the supposed containment line his crew had been cutting, the canyon continued to erupt in a thunderhead of smoke.

"Anyone hurt?" Derek called. "That was a close one! Fuck, Stoltz," he said as Mike approached, "you damn near bought it." Then, "Good job, Diego! Fuckin' hero material."

A still-burning fallen limb and its source, a charred and smoldering madrone near the canyon's edge, were reminders of a debt Mike could probably never pay. First time he'd had to drop and cover for real, and he didn't notice that tree, hadn't imagined it was there.

Diego was Diego Rodriguez, the guy now asleep in the bunk next to Mike in a barracks cubicle at Washington Ridge, their home camp. Asleep, like Mike should be. Wanted to be, at two fucking a.m.

The season had been brutal, even the fire pros said so, among the worst in California history. The entire camp was brain-dead exhausted, even after most of a week off. They were out again tomorrow, too, down to fucking Santa Barbara, so he wouldn't see Cass or Wes this weekend either, hadn't since goddamn June, when they'd been able to laze away a whole afternoon, picnicking on the grass and watching guys play volleyball or run around with their kids. "It's a camp all right," Wes had joked. "Careful you don't go soft."

Those memories, more than the dream, were why he was awake. Awake, in the dark of a quiet, safe building, with fifteen other guys asleep. Shit.

Mike was tough, prided himself on it, and pretty much loved this work, so physical and consuming you didn't have time to think how you'd fucked up and put yourself in prison. As for saving wildlands, houses and sometimes towns from devastation, you had to feel good about that. Sure, he knew fire was a main factor in the balance of nature, but plenty of areas did burn, and they didn't have to all burn just to prove the point. He could handle a McLoed or Pulaski as well as anyone, yet in a bad year like this you had no life except donkey work every day, and plenty of danger to go with. He'd wanted the challenge, it beat the crap out of being wedged in a tiny gray cell, but seeing Cass was what he lived for.

Normally if Diego was awake, they'd whisper back and forth a little, and you had a bond with a guy who'd saved your life that didn't come any other way. They never really brought that up anymore, not after Mike's round of public thanks on the crew bus, but it was always there. And they were tight enough now that Mike could even wake Diego if he needed to, but tonight would be cruel. The guy was going through hell himself, hadn't slept much any night since that letter from his dad showed up.

Twelve years younger than Mike, and just as strong, Diego had been raised by his dad in a rough north Sacramento neighborhood. Mom a druggie, long gone and likely not still alive, dad an illegal who'd built a business as a shade-tree mechanic and could fix anything from lawn mowers to Mercedes. But tenacious and loyal, he had supported his son right through high school and an earlier legal scrape into a grunt mechanic job at Qwik Lube, until the cops found the trunk of Diego's red Camaro full of stolen electronics equipment.

Yet dad hadn't abandoned him then, either. He was afraid, due to lack of papers, to visit Diego in any county or state lockup, but sent frequent, short letters that guaranteed his son a roof and fresh start when he got out. Until the most recent one, waiting for Diego when their crew got back from the fire in Mendocino, where they'd gone after Buzzard Point. Yanking the motor out of a Toyota pickup, his dad had herniated two disks, was immobilized, couldn't work, had lost the tiny rental Diego grew up in, and for the moment was laid out on the floor of a friend's place in a burg called Woodland, with nowhere to turn.

Holding the scribbled page, Diego openly cried, right there in his bunk. "Fuck!" he said, choking on tears. "I should be there. Fuck me! Locked up you can't help nobody!"

Mike could relate. He'd been under lock that whole damn spring when Beryl Watson had run Cass out of Lamoille trying to slip her his pork. "Lo siento, bro," he said, practicing a Spanish phrase Diego had taught him. "Been there."

"You gotta know him," Diego insisted, pounding the mattress with his fist. "Proud like nobody you've seen. Would whack me for crying. Must've fucking killed him to write these words. To me...his own son."

"It's a crusher," Mike said. "For a while last year I hated the guards and every cop who'd brought me in."

"I hated 'em too. Till my dad sounded off. 'Only thing worse than cops,'" he wrote in big block letters, "'is no cops.' And to him, part of no cops is bad cops. Like the ones who burned his village in Michoacán."

"Whoa," Mike said. "Never thought of it that way."

"Here's what else he says, hammered on it since I was a kid. "You take care of your own." Diego gasped out more tears. "Got that, Mike? You take care of your own."

"Ten more months, you're out, right? Eyes on the prize. For now, be creative. Who else around there can help him?"

Four nights later, Diego was at least asleep, not sighing and rustling in the dark like he had been, when nothing Mike said or did seemed to help. Wouldn't talk by day either, just brooded, and barely shrugged at the announcement about Santa Barbara.

So maybe tonight was Mike's turn to stew. Whatever, he had to take a leak, but on the way back, holy shit! Diego was quiet because of no Diego! Blankets rolled up and pulled high on the pillow to make his bunk look occupied, except the half-moon had now snuck around to the window and most of Diego's stuff was gone too. They'd all packed right after dinner to be ready for morning travel, but this looked serious.

Not that simply leaving the barracks was a big risk. Guys would sometimes do it for an afterhours smoke. You weren't supposed to, but the buildings weren't locked or under close watch. There was no continuous perimeter fence either. Pretty much an honor system when it came to rules, although head counts three times a day were mandatory.

Every few years some fool wandered off, but the word was they never got far. Prisoners were city boys, mostly, didn't know the area, and would usually be spotted and picked up, hungry and bedraggled out along Highway 20. But that wouldn't be Diego. He was too smart and had food and gear in hand. And they all kept a little cash.

The two of them used to walk the camp property on days off. There were some good views overlooking the South Fork and the rest of the Yuba drainage, and Diego had been a sponge for whatever Mike knew about it. Which was a lot. Mineral Creek backed up to the hazy blue ridgeline on the north horizon that marked the Plumas County border.

But Jesus, you want hassle? Try a failed escape. Your sentence at least doubled, a Level 4 lockup, in with the real bad asses, privileges revoked and forget about parole, fire camp or anything else. Fugitive life was no picnic either. Across the state line, Mike had lucked out with Cass, but the paranoia and constant lying sucked. Besides, Diego's dad would be the first lead they'd follow. How the hell did Diego imagine he could disappear and help at the same time? On top of everything, his old man could end up deported.

But Jesus again. The upside. A rippling sense of it coursed through him. To be free. To see Cass this weekend after all. To fuck like there was no tomorrow. Mike had never let the idea take hold, especially not here, where the potential was obvious. And now, anything to slam his mind on that before it made him crazy. He looked at his packed duffle bag on the floor. Ready. Waiting.

He got up, slipped on his prison-blue pants and shirt, picked up his boots and tip-toed out of the partitioned cubicle, past a few other bunks to the door. He knew exactly where Diego had gone. It hadn't hit him at first, but in that moment it did. The camp's northwest corner, perched above the river. Plenty of poison oak there, but he and Diego were immune. Maybe from the Native American blood they both had. That's what they'd joked when they met the day camp opened, one of the things that drew them together.

Mike took pains to avoid the moonlight, moving from shadow to shadow across the grounds into the woods. Most of the underbrush had been cleared away; fire camps made it a point to model best practice, so walking quietly and in a fairly direct route wasn't a problem. He stayed alert for any trace of Diego. Nothing.

What could Mike even do out here in the barely visible oaks, pines and madrones, shout the guy's name? That would be nuts, attract the attention of staff, make it impossible for Diego to change his mind, and probably bring down shit on Mike besides. To his right, a large pine trunk with a sign, black on yellow. He couldn't read the words but knew what they said: 'RESTRICTED AREA - Camp Boundary 25 Feet,' along with fine print threatening anyone who crossed through with some number-dot-number of the penal code. Every ten yards or so, facing in and out around the property, were trees with identical signage.

Then, at the boundary itself, sometimes a staked run of six-foot barbed wire, also signed, especially closer to the highway, and sometimes no fence at all, where drop-offs or other natural features created a barrier. The idea was as much to keep hikers and hunters out as keep prisoners in.

The unfenced corner Mike was headed to ended at a steep, brushy ravine, streambed dry at this time of year. Weeks ago, by chance, he and Diego had seen the shoulders and heads of people carrying inner tubes on a hidden path that wound down the far side, probably to reach a canyon swimming hole. The Yuba was famous for them. And across the water, a through trail would take you east or west, with connections to everywhere from Marysville to Quincy. Going west Diego could even float his gear on an improvised raft, ottering along faster than any foot pursuit. But a trail-wise guy like Mike could make good time heading east too.

And goddamn, in the filtered light at the ravine's edge, broken brush and skid-marks, clearly fresh, showed where Diego had gone. The son-of-a-bitch was free! For however long he lasted. But free was the exciting part. You never knew how or when or if it would end, which put a charge in anything you did. Mike found a low, rocky outcrop and sat, feet dangling above Diego's downhill tracks.

Now that he knew the right spot, it would take less than ten minutes to get his own gear and follow. Fire-crew duffles also worked as backpacks. All he'd have to do was adjust the carry handles. Suddenly, it was as though he could feel the thing against his shoulders and had the power to charge batteries just by touching them. Across the ravine an owl started a long, steady call.

He got up and headed toward the barracks at a careful trot. Yeah, he actually could be at Mineral Creek in three days. But Cass would never forgive him. Never. Neither would Wes. Neither would Joe. Neither would Mike himself. He wouldn't rat out Diego, no chance of that, but Mike needed to be back in his bunk before anyone noticed. Before anyone could say he might have been in on Diego's plan. Mike heard the owl again and wondered if they really were wise.

Bill Pieper, a member of the Squaw Valley Community of Writers, writes and lives in Sacramento, California. His stories have appeared in print and online in venues such as Farallon Review, Red Fez, Chiron Review, Scarlet Leaf Review *and* Front Porch Review, *with two of them receiving Pushcart nominations. Links to his 2014 collection* Forgive Me, Father *from Cold River Press and his other published work can be found at: http://www.authorsden.com/billpieper*

Outside Looking In
by Meera Ekkanath Klein

All her life Beulah Dev wanted to be somebody else.

When she was five years old, her mother was horrified to discover Beulah in their front yard, her face and hair smothered in muddy ditch water.

"You naughty, naughty girl," her mother said, pinching her arms painfully. "What are you doing?"

"Mama, I want to be Indian," Beulah had cried. "I want to be brown like everyone else."

She had cried even more wildly as her mother viciously washed the dirt out of her ginger colored hair.

"You are not Native," her mother forcefully said the word with a capital N. "You are a British lady."

Beulah knew they weren't really British. All the Europeans lived in fancy houses with cars and drivers while she shared a miserable two-room shack with her mother on the outskirts of town. Their neighbors were lower middle class Indians or other Anglo-Indians, trying hard to be as English as possible.

"Bee-bee," her mother said, "Have some bread and peanut butter."

Her mother believed her homemade peanut butter solved all problems. It was true it improved the taste of the stale dry bread with rich nutty deliciousness. It was a rare treat to get a bite of the homemade spread for mother guarded her jars of nut butter with a jealous eye. These jars were their only means of livelihood. Every Sunday her mother would make her way to the open-air bazaar and buy baskets of fresh peanuts. She would spend the day hulling the nuts and then dry roasting them in a large iron wok. On Monday she ground the nuts into a delicious spread. This was back-breaking work and Beulah was careful never to disturb her mother while she was grinding and roasting peanuts. The first and only time she had interrupted her mother she had received a quick smack on her bottom.

The nut butter was stored in recycled Horlicks bottles after each jar was washed in boiling water.

"We have to keep some standards," she would say, wiping her sweaty forehead with the back of her hand. "These Natives have no idea of sterilization and cleanliness."

A dresser drawer served as a pantry and was soon filled with jars of golden peanut butter.

Tuesday was delivery day. Before Beulah enrolled in kindergarten, she would accompany her mother on her deliveries. First stop was a big house with a tiled roof and a pretty rose garden. Beulah and her mother would go to the back of the house and tap on the door. The housekeeper, a dour woman in a cotton sari, would come out and take a jar. She would slam the door and go back inside. Beulah and her mother would wait patiently for a while and then her mother would tap on the wooden door again. The housekeeper would come out, make an exasperated face, and hand over a few rupee notes. Beulah's mother always thanked the woman who never said a word to them. Going to this house always made Beulah feel as unwanted as the old bitch dog that wandered the streets looking for a scrap of food and a kind word.

The next delivery was Beulah's favorite. Here a couple of old British ladies lived in a small cottage overrun with cats. They would invite Beulah and her mother in and offer tea and biscuits which her mother always refused with a sniff. Beulah eyed the ginger biscuits and waited until one of the women, smiling kindly, offered her a wafer. Beulah smiled back shyly as she nibbled on the sweet treat.

"We love your butter," one of the British women

would say. "It brings us a taste of home."

"Yes, home," her mother would say with a pinched look about her mouth. "It is far away."

When they were walking away from the house Beulah asked her mother, "Mama, why don't we ever have tea?"

Her mother looked down at her, "They are not our kind of people."

"But they are proper British ladies, who want to be our friends. It must be nice to have a good friend," Beulah's voice was wistful.

"No, they are not proper anything. I sell them my butter but I draw the line at having tea with such women."

"Why mama?"

"Enough talk about those deviant ladies. They are of no concern to us."

Beulah didn't say anything more but she wondered why her mother was so angry at the two women and what deviant meant.

At the next delivery Beulah had to sit on the front porch while her mother went inside with a couple of jars of nut butter. She knew an Englishman called "the colonel" lived here. The one time she had seen him, his bulging gooseberry colored eyes had frightened her. His pink wet lips had made her want to go home and wash her hands.

"Wait here and don't run around," her mother said before disappearing into the house.

It seemed like a long time before she came out with her breath smelling funny like when she sipped from a bottle of gin she kept in the back cupboard for "medicinal purposes."

"Your blouse is buttoned wrong Mama," Beulah said.

"Hush," her mama said as she hurriedly re-buttoned the blouse. "Let's go home."

Once Beulah started school she no longer went on these delivery trips with her mother. She missed the two British cat ladies and their ginger biscuits.

During lunch Beulah nibbled on her sandwich, avoiding the dry and stale edges. She watched with envy as the Indian girls ate hot lunches, delivered by servant girls. The fragrance from the steaming mounds of rice, pungent gravy and garlic broth brought tears of longing to Beulah's eyes. Beulah yearned for a taste of the hot lunch as much as she wished for the girls' smooth brown complexion and sleek black braids. Her ginger colored curls never stayed in place, no matter how tightly her mother braided the unwieldy locks.

One day while she was eyeing the creamy curd rice and bits of fiery red mango pickle, one of the Indian girls saw her interest.

"Want to try a pickle?" she asked, holding out a bit of oily mango.

"Why do you want to bother with the dingo?" her friend said. "Her pale tongue can't handle our spice."

Those words forced Beulah to defiantly hold out her hand and accept the mango bit. The piece of pickled vegetable was salty, hot and delicious. Even though Beulah's eyes watered and her mouth and tongue burned from the chili peppers, she smiled and nodded her thanks.

"Mama, what's a dingo?" she asked her mother later that day.

Her mother was busy pouring her version of soup, a bland broth of soggy vegetables, into cracked china bowls. She paused when she heard Beulah's question.

"Where did you hear that?"

"One of the girls called me a dingo. Am I a dingo?"

Her mother put down the soup and hugged her fiercely.

"You are not a dingo," she whispered against Beulah's curls. "You are English and one day when we have enough money we will go back to England and leave this wretched country behind."

Her mother quietly said, "You can have some peanut butter on your bread tonight."

It was only late at night that she realized her mother had never answered her question. She thought about what her mother had said about being them being British.

Perhaps she would belong with the British girls with their pale complexions and flaxen colored hair. So one day she joined the group, hovering on the outskirts, unsure of her welcome.

"What do you want?" a tall thin girl with bright red hair asked in a very proper British accent.

"Nothing," Beulah whispered.

"Then bugger off, will you?" the girl said and turned her back on her.

"Alright, I will," Beulah said in a rare show of spirit. "You, dingo, you."

The minute the words were out of her mouth she knew she had said something terribly wrong and insulting.

"What the devil did you call me?" the redhead asked in an icy voice. "Look here, you..."

The girl was so angry she was lost for words.

"Listen," a blonde spoke up, not unkindly. "You better learn not to say these things to us. We are after all British."

The redhead had found her voice, "Yes, you are the dirty little dingo, smelling like peanuts. Get out of here, you half breed."

That's when Beulah realized that a dingo was a person like her, someone who didn't fit into any world. She was an eternal outsider. She longed to belong but her mixed blood was a living curse. She had looked up the word dingo in a dictionary at school. *A wild dog with reddish yellow fur.*

Maybe like a wild dog she didn't belong in normal society. She was doomed to wander the outer fringes, afraid to enter and yet too frightened to take off on her own. That moment defined her solitary childhood and set her apart from her classmates.

As she neared adolescence, Beulah's unusual curls and creamy golden complexion attracted the attention of boys. One group of boys, who attended the neighboring all-boys school, took to following her and taunting her with remarks.

Every afternoon, Beulah dreaded the walk home, looking for a way to escape the rowdy boys. One particularly bold boy tried to touch her curls.

"They are like ginger roots gone wild," he said.

Beulah had brushed his hands off feeling a little frightened and angry.

"Come on, Miss Ginger Hair," he said. "You Anglo-Indian girls are all alike teasing a fellow with your fair skin and leading him on."

Beulah had no idea what he was talking about and so began to walk faster. The boy continued to follow her. In a fright, Beulah began to run. That is when it happened. Her legs seemed to take on a life of their own and soon she was far ahead of the pack of boys.

She found different paths, some taking her through crowded neighborhoods. Beulah ran uphill and downhill, but she never paused. She just ran and ran until she was no longer little Beulah with ginger curls and peanut breath. She was a well-oiled running machine with pistons for legs and oxygen filled lungs. Soon she was soaring away, light as a feather. When she was moving like this, Beulah was no longer an outsider, a dingo. All those outsider feelings tumbled out and disappeared into thin air. With each powerful exhalation Beulah felt every rejection and heart ache leave her body until all that was left was a puff of air, soft as a zephyr.

Meera Ekkanath Klein loves to cook and write and so it was only natural that she combined both these passions in her first award-winning book My Mother's Kitchen: A Novel with Recipes. *Klein lives in Davis where she is currently working on several writing projects.*

by Gayle Jansen Beede

89

Morton Gets The Picture
by Dorothy Place

The first and last time I saw her was at an art gallery on West Broadway at the opening of an exhibition of wire sculptures. She had a sun-blushed look that gave her skin and hair an aura of honesty not often seen in New York City. I knew she would smell like freshly plowed earth after a light morning rain. If you believe in love at first sight, then you'll believe me when I say I was smitten.

She was standing next to a tall thin guy with long dirty-blonde hair into which a purple ribbon had been braided. He was dressed in black, wore a beret, and clutched a magenta leather jacket that had been tossed carelessly over his left shoulder. Right away I pegged him as Nicki Norwood, the artist featured on the poster outside the gallery. I could tell his type a mile off. The kind of guy who insisted his work wasn't commercial. I knew what "commercial" meant. Even with a fabricated name like Nicki Norwood, he wasn't selling anything.

He was standing before a small group of art patrons and pointing to a sculpture that looked something like a huge tangle of wires that had been yanked out of a telephone circuit box by an exasperated technician and thrown onto a flagpole that was angling forward at about thirty degrees. It didn't look like anything I could identify, and the notes in the exhibit catalog weren't any help. It was labelled, *Flight of the Gallows*. It didn't look like any gallows I had ever seen, and it was hardly flight-worthy. I couldn't believe anyone would purchase it. Not for $2,500. But then, I'm no art critic. I was there for the wine and cheese. I moved closer so I could hear what this Norwood character was saying.

"It's the total ramification of the composition," he said, nodding toward the sun-blushed beauty. "And once the potential of its immutability is realized, the viewer can see where the externalities gather into the organic interior and form a matrix that descends into nothingness." As he spoke, his right hand swept from the apex of the work toward the floor.

She smiled and her eyes sparkled with amazement, as if his analysis had brought about an extraordinary revelation. Her luscious lips parted, showing perfect teeth.

Sweet Jesus. I had heard that kind of art babble before and she, innocent and totally hooked, was buying all that garbage.

Being a habitué of the New York art world's Friday night openings, I could spot a phony at a hundred yards. They're all alike: arty dress, flamboyant gestures, over-the-top articulation. Perhaps I was the one honest person who could rescue her from becoming lost in this wilderness of pretense.

The Norwoods of the art world are a formidable bunch, well loved by the art-loving groupies who can't make heads or tails out of what they're viewing. Fans are pleased to have someone explain to them the significance of each piece and, feeling enlightened, they murmur things in return about the depth of the artists' message. Somehow, I had to get between this pretentious fool and the innocent standing beside him. But, before I took this guy on, I needed some fortification. I stuck my empty wine glass behind a bunch of wires wrapped around a polished hulk of black granite called *Medusa in the Mirror* and pushed my way toward the wine bar.

"Red or white?" the hostess asked. She wore a green and red plaid cape, a black velvet Rembrandt-style hat, and black-rimmed glasses. Her Goth make-up translated her face into a charcoal drawing.

"Let me see." I examined the labels on the wine bottles as if I were a connoisseur and this was my first rather than fourth trip for refreshments that night. "Perhaps the white." I pointed to the bottle with the most appealing label.

A ghoulishly white hand appeared out of a slit in the cape, grabbed the bottle of Chardonnay by the neck, and poured. I winked, swirled the wine, and sniffed.

"Hey, Lover boy, step aside," the hostess groused, sticking some stray strands of hair into her floppy hat and jerking her head sideways. "This ain't no wine tasting." She turned to the man next in line and asked, "Red or white?" He brushed against me as he leaned forward, pushing me aside.

"Excuse me," I said, grabbing a few cubes of cheese and stashing them in my pocket along with the others I had taken earlier that evening. The crowd had thickened so it took several minutes before I located my sun-blushed beauty. An art object herself, she was standing in the center of a large group, her face lightly flushed and her hands joined behind as if she were little Alice searching Wonderland for the key to making her big. Norward was still with her and still nattering on.

As far as art goes, my taste runs to the pictures in comic books rather than the abstract stuff you see in SoHo galleries. The collection in my apartment consists of a couple of Peter Max reprints I inherited from the previous tenant, a Maltese Falcon movie poster I found in a second hand store on Second Avenue, and two Bill Blass t-shirts I bought over on Seventh Avenue. Probably knock offs. But when you have nothing else to do on a Friday night and you're feeling lonely, art openings are about as good as it gets in the city: free food and wine, fascinating people to look at, and sometimes even a glimpse of art that says more to you than "Guess what I am!"

I tossed a chunk of cheese into my mouth and started toward the group still standing in front of the ball of wires caught on the end of a flagpole. What more could Norward be saying about that piece of junk left high and dry by a passing utility truck?

Just then, my eye caught someone pushing her way toward me. "Sweet Jesus save me," I muttered.

"Spinky," one of my past mistakes called out, her long green and white tie-dyed shirt fluttering over her knit tights. "Over here." Her arm was flailing in what could be interpreted as a beckoning motion. As she hurried toward me, I could see the rhinestones in the chain holding her reading glasses winking at the overhead lights and hear the jangle of her wrist-to- mid-arm bracelets.

Spinky isn't my name. It's what she insisted on calling me after we'd had too much wine at the art opening on Greene Street two Fridays ago and ended up in her apartment in the Village, ostensibly for me to comment on the work she had recently turned out in her water color class. She'd wanted me to believe she was what she called an "emerging artist," but we both knew she wanted to get me into the sack. That's another freebie I forgot to mention. These Friday night art openings are the spawning grounds for newly divorced women trying out their recently acquired sexual freedom. And I am not averse to helping them out.

"Why didn't you call me?" she asked, grabbing my arm and holding it close to her side. I could feel her excess plump boiling over her Spanks. "You promised," she whimpered. Her eyelids lowered in a hurt sort of way, and her lips pushed forward like she was expecting a kiss.

"Lost your number," I lied. The nerve endings in my arm telegraphed the shape of the fat rolls around her midsection to my memory bank, reminding me of that night of groaning and sweating on her Sleep-Number bed. That's all you can do when you're caught. Lie. Unfortunately, even as you say the words, you know you're digging deeper. But what could I do? Lament my deep morning-after remorse? Explain that I had hoped our paths would never cross again? Admit that I couldn't even remember her name? Hypocrisy, as usual, won out. "I hoped you'd be here tonight," I said softly, trying my best to sound sincere.

"You wouldn't be putting me on, would you?" She raised her eyebrows and gave me an unrelenting stare that said she didn't believe one word. "I saw you put my number in your cell."

I squirmed a bit and then blurted, "Lost my cell." There it was. A quick cover up that put me in deeper. The only thing left was to pray the damned phone wouldn't ring.

Norwood saved me. He was leading his small army of admirers over to the art work by which my Friday night mistake and I were standing. He eased himself in front of us and immediately began speaking.

"Now this one," he said, gesturing toward a bunch of wires bound tightly into the shape of an upward thrusting something closely resembling a gigantic phallic symbol, "is probably the most innovative piece being shown tonight, as it embodies both the physical and emotional side of the human condition." The group hummed and nodded. Encouraged, he added, "You might say it contains both the tangible and the intangible elements of existence." As he spoke, he nodded toward the delicious little tidbit I had been admiring and held out his hand toward her.

Watching him perform in front of that outsized piece of rock in full tumescence while attempting to make physical contact with her made my blood pressure rise. My fists curled into two tightly drawn weapons and I vowed that, if he put a hand on her, I'd punch him in the face. As I assessed how well my 155 pounds would do against his six-foot frame, my Friday night mistake ago grabbed the hand Norwood held out and squeezed it against her breasts.

"Oh my," she said, her purple eyelids looking like she needed a hunk of beefsteak to heal them, "that was the most erudite observation I have ever heard." For some reason, her heaving breasts set loose under that green and white shirt made me think of the sea upon which the owl and the pussy

94

cat had set themselves adrift. I struggled to keep from laughing, but my attention quickly shifted to the fact that Norwood was, at this moment, uncharacteristically speechless. It was great seeing two phonies come face-to-face. Calming, I tried to guess which one was going to out-bullshit the other.

"Errr, yes," Norward stammered. "I can see you are truly an art aficionado." He bowed slightly and grimaced as he lowered his leather jacket from his shoulder, using one hand to steady himself on the sculpture's platform and the other to pry loose her fingers. But as soon as his hand was free, my Friday night mistake grabbed his arm and, using her ample hip, maneuvered him away from the group, chatting about art. Norwood looked back over his shoulder, his eyes pleaded for help. I felt quite smug, as though I had arranged the whole thing and had rid myself of two impediments with one blow.

Bewildered by the turn of events, the group muttered among themselves and slowly dissolved. I grabbed the opportunity and stepped into the void. "Shall we take a breather and go for a glass of wine?" I asked. She nodded, so I took her elbow and propelled her toward the bar.

As we made our way through the crowd, several of the art patrons smiled and made comments to her about the collection. "Exquisite showing," an older guy with a Mensa logo pinned to his purple vest called out. He was pushing toward us through a knot of patrons, but before he could intercept our progress, I jockeyed our way through a small space between a palm tree and an announcement board. Now that I had her to myself, I wasn't going to let anyone spoil my chances.

"White or red?" I asked as we approached the bar.

"I'll just have water."

"A white and a glass of water," I said to Rembrandt Hat.

"Are you going to put something in the tip jar this time?" she asked.

I pulled out one of my last dollars and handed it to her.

"In the jar." She pointed her chin in the direction of a mason jar filled with money and handed me the drinks.

As we turned from the bar, I suggested we find a place where we could talk.

Smiling, she took a sip of water and looked around. "I really should stay out on the floor. You understand, of course."

I got it. She was the gallery receptionist. She was on the job. That explained why she was so patient with Norwood, why so many seemed to know her, and why she was drinking water instead of wine.

Just as I was about to get down to business, a woman with a huge diamond and sapphire tree-of-life brooch at her neck, a cane, and a catalog for the exhibit shouldered herself between us. "My dear," she said, turning her back to me and speaking directly to my sun-blushed beauty, "this is the most extraordinary exhibit I've seen in SoHo this season. Congratulations."

"How nice of you to say. It took a while to get it together. Did you get a signed catalog?"

I was wrong. She was not the receptionist. She was the curator for the exhibit. I struggled to see beyond the backside of Mrs. Ostentatious Brooch. There was Norwood, across the room, lecturing another small group. My Friday night mistake was not to be seen. I wondered how he had gotten rid of her.

"Are you working on anything else?" the Ostentatious Brooch asked.

"Not at the moment," my sweet thing answered. "But I have some ideas."

"Anything you want to tell me?" The woman raised her eyebrows and leaned forward, eager to get the latest art-world scoop.

"No. But Mrs. Graham, you'll be one of the first to get a notice for my next opening."

"I'm looking forward to it," the woman said. "Oh,

there's Michael!" She hurried off, chasing after the mayor.

I decided to make my move. "Maybe after this is over tonight you can come to my place and see my collection."

"Are you a collector?"

"Modest," I said, wondering how some reprints and a couple of knockoff t-shirts could be passed off as a collection. Worry about that later, I told myself. Get her up there first.

"What are you interested in?"

I rocked back on my heels and concocted what I thought might be a bemused expression. "Some modern. But this kind of stuff leaves me cold."

"Oh," she said.

Her disappointment was palpable; I was on shaky ground. She'd organized the show, so she must have a lot invested in it. How could I be so stupid? Too negative and there went my chances. "I meant, not usually interested in abstractions. But this," I said, waving my hand around, "is— is—different. Yes, that's it. This stuff is very—unusual you might say. Unusual and quite provocative." I looked at her closely, hoping I had recovered some ground.

"Hmmm," she said, her brown eyes searching my face. "What do you mean by provocative?"

Oh boy. In it again. Provocative. I bounced on my toes, giving myself some time to think. "I'm not an expert," I began, "so—well, it's hard for me to say. But you. You're the expert. Why don't you help me understand what I'm seeing?"

She took my arm, and walked me over to the sculpture of *Medusa in the Mirror.* "This is one of my favorites." She gently touched the column on which the piece rested.

"I can see why," I nodded and tried to sound as though I was reaching deep down to find the meaning hidden in this pile of granite wrapped in wires. I wasn't coming up with anything.

"Really? What do you see in it?"

She wasn't making this easy. I cast around and decided to give her my first impression. That's what I'd heard some critics say. Go with your guts. But to tell the truth, all I saw was a big rock and some wires. I rubbed my chin and realized I had been at the gallery too long. My beard was growing back.

"Relax and just tell me what you see," she coaxed. "It really isn't that difficult."

"Well, I can see that the wires are Medusa's hair and—and the rock probably represents the old gal herself. And black, of course, is the very essence of the composition." Essence. I couldn't believe I came up with that word. But it worked. She was smiling and nodding.

Blown away by my own bullshit, I asked, "But where's the mirror?"

"Here," she said, resting her hand on the granite.

"But I thought the hunk of rock was Medusa."

"You're right," she said. "When Medusa looked into the mirror, she saw herself and turned to stone. All that's left is her hair."

I searched my memory and grabbed some of Norwood's words. "Very organic," I said. "And somewhat immutable." She shrugged and looked away. I could see she wasn't impressed, so I decided to be up front with her. "Okay. So the rock is Medusa. But I'm still puzzled. I just don't see the mirror."

"Well, it would have seen what Medusa saw, but in reverse. Right?"

"Right."

"So, seeing Medusa, the mirror turned to stone, too." Her eyes searched mine for some hint of understanding.

"You mean everything turned to stone except her hair?"

She nodded. "You got it."

"Why not that, too?"

"Because the hair is immune," she answered. "You see, it can't turn to stone because it's the embodiment of the curse."

I shook my head. "Sounds like a bunch of crap that man-in-black with the beret was spouting." Ouch! That was the wine talking, but I couldn't stop now that I got started. "To me, it's just a bunch of wires and a black rock."

Her shocked expression quickly vanished, but not before it signaled that I had committed a *faux pas* from which I was not easily going to recover. "I can see what you're saying," she murmured. Her voice was apologetic, as if she had been the socially inept one. "You've discovered the viewer's fascination with modern art, how it draws the person in and allows him to stretch his mind. Everyone sees something different. And because they see it differently, everyone's interpretation is right. It's all very personal." She gave me one of her glowing smiles.

Diplomatic. Just like a curator. Never turn off a customer, no matter how obnoxious he is. You never know where the next sale might be coming from. "You may be right, but do you think anyone will put up any dough for this stuff?"

"I hope so. As one critic said, writing a check is so much more sincere than writing a review."

The thought of writing a check for one of these pieces took me by surprise. Was she thinking I'd buy something? "I need another drink," I said and walked to the wine bar.

When I returned she was once more standing like an art object among a bunch of admirers, giving them her thoughts on the Medusa and the mirror stuff. I stood at the edge of the group feeling sorry for her. No matter how hard she tried, she was never going to sell any of Norwood's junk. I wondered what my chances of making a comeback were. Perhaps an apology? Plead ignorance?

My thoughts were interrupted by Norwood. He had walked up to the group and was standing next to me. "She's something, isn't she?" he asked. He was looking at her like he owned her.

I wanted to tell him what a fraud he was but it was getting late and, after my sixth glass of wine, my words weren't lining up. I nodded and buried my nose in my glass, trying to figure out how I was going to get rid of him and if I had enough time to make amends for my rudeness.

When she heard Norwood's voice, she turned and smiled broadly. "There you are," she said, giving him a wave. "I thought you tired and went home early."

"Ready for supper, Nicki?" he asked. "I made nine o'clock reservations for the Bloombergs and us at Gothams. Michael is thinking of getting one of your pieces for his office at city hall."

I looked from her to him. "Nicki?" I mumbled. While I was trying to figure it out, she turned to the group and said, "I have to go now." As she slowly disengaged herself, I could hear her saying, "Thanks, thanks so much for coming." She took the arm of the man I thought was Norwood and, as she passed me she whispered, "Next time, I hope you get the picture.

Since submitting her first short story in 2008, Dorothy Place has had thirteen short stories accepted for publication in literary journals; four have been awarded prizes or recognition, and one, a fellowship. Her debut, literary fiction novel, The Heart To Kill, *has been published by SFA Press (2016) and released November 2016. The manuscript for a collection of fifteen short stories won the Jameson Award at the Blue Moon Literary Conference.*

Cat & Mouse

An excerpt from a memoir, *Reminiscence,*
by David Lloyd Sutton

The sand of Chu Lai was dazzling white, glinting in
the sun that filled the sky. Twenty or so of us sat on the face
of a long dune and listened to an Infantry Corporal from the
battalion we were relieving lecture on avenues of approach to
the wire, enemy activity, and just what holding this particular
line entailed. Out seventy-five or a hundred meters beyond
the triple concertina perimeter fence there was a channel, and
some sort of vegetation, maybe tamarisks, but the heat shim-
mer and dust haze made it hard to make out details. Much
farther out, dust rose from vehicular and equipment activity. To our right there was a slumped bunker of sun-bleached
sandbags, some of them split and spilling their contents ...
oddly, yellower sand than that we sat on.

I had just noticed the disparity in sand color when the
sand immediately in front of *me* kicked up, and the sound of
a round fired from that channel reached us as the bullet that
had narrowly missed *me* slobbered off into the distance. I
had been highest up the dune, and the farthest from the bunker, and apparently the biggest target. There was a shoving
cluster of men at the tiny entry port...I turned, slipping in
the sand, and went the other way, sprinting for a section of
old discarded tank tread, the only other possible cover for
hundreds of feet. My Lieutenant reached it first, intelligently
not having gone for the bunker at all. I flopped flat in the
open, fountaining sand, yanking my M14's bolt to chamber a
round, and heard sand grate in the action. Still, I slapped the

bolt pull with the heel of my palm, seating the gritty round, and sought over my peep sight for someone to shoot with it. Nothing. I was scared and I really wanted to kill someone, but...Nothing.

After a few minutes, the lecture resumed, though no one but me took their chambered rounds out or stopped peering for targets while the Corporal talked. I was busy for a bit cleaning my chamber and wiping down rounds. I have wondered for years whether that was a Cong sniper drifted in from the RMK BRJ construction site out about two thousand meters from our front, as the corporal suggested, or whether our predecessors had set up an alertness drill for us, like the grenade range staff had, back in ITR. I doubt it, because if we'd had a grenade launcher among us, that channel would have been full of shrapnel.

Five of us had that collapsing bunker for the night. We were directed to conduct walking patrols, singly, on each watch; something else that shouldn't have happened, and wouldn't have, if our predecessors had remained on-site for a transition experience-sharing. A moving guard on a known line is just a moving target. But we were all new at this. I was only mildly doubtful as I set out on my patrol of several hundred meters of line.

I was still stripped above the waist, wore that floppy bush hat, a layer of the futile mosquito repellant, carefully *not* on the reddened patches inside my elbows or under my arms, where it had already burned me, weapons belt, trousers, and boots. I wore the boots only because of the tiny sand asps, which, we had been informed, just that morning, would bite you between the toes and kill you dead in about three screaming hours. I never saw one. If I hadn't belatedly remembered reading about them in a herpetology book back at Hansen's library I would have suspected something on the order of a Snipe hunt. More immediately, bare feet left one with abraded between-toes skin because the sand *was* crystalline and the grains were sharp. Most of us had gone about in our shower flip-flops or bare feet the first day, for coolness, before the medics warned everyone about the asps. Most of us had raw feet as a result.

It was like being *in* a Bonestell illustration of the moon's surface. The Milky Way, a broad foamy ribbon, lay across depthless black sky; a rising full moon cast stark shadows between dunes, made the sweeping curves and rippled slip faces glow white. That moon, still in horizon-birth, was magnified by the lens of atmosphere. Moon and sand seemed to be one surface. Occasional sparse bushes were the only vegetation, and soon I wrapped my rifle with cammy burlap I'd had stuffed in a pocket, gingerly sprinkled my repellant-sticky skin with pinches of sand to kill reflection, and settled in alongside one of those bushes. After that afternoon I was *not* going to move around like a target in a moonlit shooting gallery. I scooped sand over feet and legs to blend better. From this position I could see all of the line I was responsible for, save a hundred feet or so at either end, where the bunkers would have visual coverage.

I held very still, entranced with the lunar landscape around me and a sense of at last being where I had wanted to be for so long. The world was a beautiful place.

A loud, screeching croak just behind me brought me exploding out of the sand, clicking my safety off, whirling in mid-air to confront...a *lizard*, about eighteen inches long, with a domed skull the size of a squirrel's, its body language seeming to express mild astonishment at my antics. When I had brought my incipient heart attack under control, I thought, *What a weird place. Silent birds, salt water wells, and singing lizards.*

The operatic lizard meandered off about its lizardly affairs, I turned to resume my vigil, and, outlined by headlights from the heart of the enclave a couple of miles away, I saw a cat's silhouette on top of the fence. I almost said, "Heere, Kitty"... the way I would have on guard back stateside, in hopes the cat was friendly and would let me pet it. Then I realized a number of things very rapidly:

1. That "fence" was triple coils of concertina barbed wire, one coil centered on top of two, about twenty-two feet tall, a sloping glacis of rigid strands on engineer stakes on the outside; the whole assembly wider than it was high.

2. This "kitty" had a sloping forehead, a projecting muzzle, a non-fluffy curving tail, and a very long body. My kitty was a tiger.

3. It was a very *big* tiger, because it had to be at least two hundred yards out to be visible across the top coil.

4. The tiny land-sea breeze was from me to the cat.

Just as my stumbling thoughts reached point 4, the tiger turned its head, raised its nose, and I saw its chest grow thicker. It was inhaling deeply. Then it *looked* at me. The tiger strode fluidly into a shadow and vanished.

I had read Jim Corbett's *Man Eaters of Kumaon* when I was thirteen, and a couple of times since. I felt like I had just had my neck wrapped in ice, despite the actual temperature. *It's* outside *the wire. Nothing bigger than one of those lizards is going through that wire.*

I heard the crunch and squeak of compressed sand.

The dune I was on concealed a short segment of fence from me, so I took three fast steps closer, and could clearly see an impression, with settling sand already starting to fill it, just outside the wire...and a bigger impression and filling paw prints leading from it, *inside* the wire.

My bayonet's looped hilt slipped over my rifle muzzle, pommel socket snapped onto the mating lug; I flipped the 14's fire selector to full automatic, and with my right arm across my chest, high, elbow warding my throat, put muzzle and bayonet to my rear, over my shoulder. I began twirling, scrambling to get into the biggest patch of unshadowed and bush-free sand I could reach.

The unseen tiger began its hunting purr. It sounded

like a basso profundo going, "MMMMHHRRRMMMM-MMRRRRRUUUUMM," only louder by far than a human could achieve, *right between my knees.*

There were dunes, their dark shadows, and bushes between me and the bunker. Trying to regain its shelter alone would be suicide. "CORPORAL OF THE GUARD. POST NUMBER ONE!!" Absurdly, I remembered Johnson and his aged mountain lion back on Pendleton. I had an instant of retroactive sympathy.

The purr ceased only for an instant, resumed, swirling about in a directionless perfection of predatory mental warfare. I kept turning, knowing that tigers prefer to attack from behind, and like to avoid getting stuck on hoes or axes or bayonets...

"What the fuck you want, Sutton?" The irritated voice from the bunker, out of sight and at least three hundred feet away, sounded tiny. This time the purr didn't even hesitate.

"Get out here in a four-man team, with the M-60. Walk back to back. I've got a tiger trying to eat my ass!!"

"You've got to be shitting me!!" About then, though, the corporal must have heard the serenade I was being treated to, because next I heard, over the tiger's mutter, **"On our way! Try not to shoot us!"**

It took a few minutes for them to reach me, and I was getting seriously dizzy, even changing my direction of rotation frequently. Just as I spotted the three men's sidling movement, the purr ceased. I converged on them as fast as I could travel while still twirling, socketed myself into the group. "If you took any longer, you'd have found a big-assed cat needing toothpicks, dammit!"

"Quitchurbitchin. We got here, didn't we?"

I was embarrassed to realize that I had been so scared that I had called for *everyone* to come save me. The Corporal had remembered to leave a man on post. He didn't mention it to me. After some field phone calls, neither we nor any of the other bunker groups ran any more solo patrols.

106

I fell asleep in the muggy bunker, on a layer of empty C ration cartons left from months of previous use.

Two white-blotched little rats copulating on my chest woke me with their excited squeaking and sharp claws.

I actually hesitated to interrupt them. I had just had a glimpse of the world from their point of view. And at least *someone* was having fun tonight.

David Lloyd Sutton has written magazine articles on topics ranging from martial arts to horses to firearms. His short work has appeared repeatedly in Community of Voices, *an anthology associated with the Santa Barbara Writers' Conference.*

_____

Two Poems
by Paula Yup

Buried On The Family Land

I gave her an orange at the store
was it a year ago can't remember

Jimmy her father said a month ago
she had an injection and lithium

The broken window at Island Pride
his memory of her she broke it

I thought she was in Hawai'i with her brother
treatment for her psychosis

When she was in high school in the States
such bright future smartest in her class

That day a month ago Jimmy says
"She sang and danced for me. Happy girl."

Almost Christmas this sadness
the bright girl only twenty-two

Her brother came back for the funeral
he planned for her to live with him

Much too late took too long
in November she hung herself

She is buried on the family land
the concrete block in the yard

Her grandmother had such sadness
she loved her granddaughter

Her sadness took her away
the grandmother passed

I gave her an orange was it a year ago
she was hungry she said

Drowning In Relatives

the day after my sister's letter
written over a year's time
the news a brick
thrown throwaway
through the window
of my own concerns
I do not want to know

My cousin Amy in Hong Kong
the policeman I met
over thirty years ago
on dialysis now
my auntie who i stayed with

now turning ninety
a cousin in Phoenix
his wife in a coma
it's a secret
a nephew in high school
came out on Facebook
my sister's son
another nephew
sleeps all day
plays videogames all night
twenty not in school
has no job
threatens suicide
angry that his ADD
not his fault
everyone else to blame
he won't move out

my niece
half white half Chinese
feels too dumb by half
her Asian friends so smart
she is stupid
will never get to college
a nephew giving up on college
graduates from basic training
for the air force
making a go at life

my brother-in-law
maxed out the credit cards
My sister dismayed
such a surprise
she just found out

couldn't get groceries
at the store
a brother had back surgery
asthma sends him
to the emergency room

my lawyer sister-in-law
quits her job
housewife again
after her teen son
has seizures
several years after
brain surgery
at John's Hopkins
for cancerous tumors
removed
a couple years ago
allowed to attend high school
after physical therapy
paralyzed on half his body

Don't know what to do
distracted by tears
numb with the news
Bonnie gives me a ride
headed to New Hope Store

Thirty-five dollars each
for four uniforms
four little girls
going back to school
instead of selling handicrafts
for their mothers

"They're not truant.
The family can't buy uniforms.

A public school.
Can you imagine!
Thirty-five dollars a uniform
the nerve of it!"
Bonnie in her element
drops me off

and I walk back
to my apartment
need the exercise
betwixt and between

almost Thanksgiving
thoughts scatter a light rain

———————————————

Paula Yup is an artist and poet who lives in Spokane, WA.

Made in the USA
San Bernardino, CA
31 May 2018